Rose

First published 2015
Second edition 2024
Copyright © Simon Cornish.

ISBN: 9798326794789

Book Design & Cover: Simon Cornish

ROSETTA

Simon Cornish

1: Cambridge and Exeter

There is a denial of finality that comes with the arrogance of youth. A consequence of the belief that we still have more time left in the world than we have already existed. At thirty-four, Graham still had enough of that hubris left to go running most days and play squash with a group of theologians and English post-grads from King's every Thursday. Today, in-fact. He'd have to call and let them know he wasn't going to be able to make it. He looked down and realised he was still holding his mobile. He pocketed it, checking the number first. It was the Professor's. The woman must have been some kind of relative, or at least a close friend. She'd sounded too emotional to simply be a solicitor or other official. It would be unlikely such a person would be using the Professor's phone anyway.

The call had caught him by surprise as he was making his way to the main hall for lunch.

"Is this Dr Chandlers, Dr Graham Chandlers? I'm..." Graham had barely been able to hear the woman's voice over the melee of students passing through the narrow college vestibule and missed catching her name.

"Just a second..." he'd said, stepping through into the comparative quiet of an adjoining seminar room and shutting the door on the bedlam.

"...Sorry about that. How can I help you?"

"The school office gave me this number. Am I interrupting anything?" Her voice had sounded husky, with an intriguing foreign inflection. He usually had a knack for placing people's accents within a few syllables, a by-product of his field of study, but an origin for hers eluded him. At his reply to the negative, she'd continued. "It's about Alan Hargreaves, he," she'd paused momentarily. "He died last night."

"What? Oh, crap. How?" Graham had turned to look through the windows. To stare out at the gardens that bordered this part of the venerable building, now in the grip of fresh spring growth, bushes and shrubs pricked with green beneath blossom laden trees that spilled pink snow into the wind. The professor had been old, but hardly elderly. Though, who knows how time had treated the man since Graham had last seen him?

"He had a stroke at the end of last week. They took him to the Royal Devon in Exeter, but he... he never woke up." she'd said, her voice catching.

"I'm genuinely sorry to hear that," he'd said. How long had it been? Eight years? Guilt had tugged at his conscience for not having made more of an effort in that time. "The Professor, Alan, was a good man," he'd said, continuing to stare at the falling petals outside, "a good friend and a great archaeologist." What could one say? There is no right thing to say when confronted with that kind of news.

"He thought a lot of you, Dr Chandlers. If you can come to the funeral service, would you consider doing

6

a –what's the word for it– a speech for him?" she'd said.

"Eulogy?" Graham had offered.

"Yes, a eulogy."

"I'd be honoured."

Graham had been due to visit his parents at the weekend, suffering his mother's gentle queries about finding a nice girl to settle down with, and his sister's more pointy jibes about how many students had thrown themselves at him this week. It was a family joke. With his green eyes and dark loosely curled hair he wasn't an unattractive man and there had been no shortage of girlfriends over the years. He had, however, drawn the line at dating undergraduates when he'd started teaching out of a sense of professional integrity. Instead, he spent the weekend in his tiny Cambridge flat attempting to finish his latest paper. It concerned how the writing process on ancient styli and clay tablets, in itself being a painstaking process, would have resulted in a more formalised version of a language that ought to differ in marked ways from that spoken every day in those ancient cultures. It cited various examples from more contemporary languages as a comparison. But, without any direct evidence of ancient speech, it would only ever remain a hypothesis. He did as much as he could, sat on the living room floor with his laptop on his crossed legs, notes fanned out around him, but the draft he managed to produce still needed work and some better citations before it would be anywhere near ready for publication. On the Monday morning he made the twenty-minute walk to his office at Corpus Christi and undertook the final arrangements to reorganise his schedule around this unexpected trip to Exeter. After lunch at the college he walked home, threw his bags into the back of the Discovery and set off.

The journey to the South West was tiring, alternating between bright sunshine and heavy falls of rain, along with bursts of speed between bouts of heavy traffic. He'd managed to get a late deal on a room at one of the better hotels in the city centre and, having negotiated the labyrinthine traffic system, checked in to the Rougemont around seven.

Rather than trying to compete with Exeter's nightlife, Graham chose to have his dinner in the hotel's calm and underpopulated restaurant. The whole Edwardian building had obviously undergone some extensive refurbishment recently and everywhere, from the bedrooms to the foyer, left the impression of tasteful perfection. The restaurant and the grilled trout he was served were no exception. Having finished, Graham fetched his notes from his room and moved on to the bar, where, with the help of a large single malt, he began to plan what he was going to say at the funeral service the following morning. Alan –Professor Alan Hargreaves to give him his full nomenclature– had been Graham's teacher, mentor and supervisor during his tenure as a student, and later, faculty member at Exeter University's archaeology department. It had been the professor, in his quiet, thoughtful way, who'd seen the bright, sometimes opinionated student's potential. Not in fitting together the four-dimensional jigsaws of dig sites, but puzzling out the nuances of characters and phonetics of long dead languages, the treasures to be found inscribed on ancient stonework, papyri and clay tablets.

Graham had brought printouts of family and biographical information about the man, used for the introduction of a jointly written book which had been published just after Graham had left the archaeology department at Exeter to take up his research fellowship at Cambridge. The professor's academic record was well-known and Graham cherry-picked the highlights, as well as a couple of fond anecdotes. Including the infamous sewage incident.

He was unsure what, if anything, he should say about the odd circumstances leading up to the professor's retirement, even though the man had only been in his early sixties at the time. It had been after his last dig in Turkey. From all accounts, a bit of a cock-up with the authorities at Ankara resulting in the team having their licence to dig withdrawn. But the professor had returned months later all fired-up about some discovery that would change the current understanding of the ancient world entirely. He'd drafted papers, even muttered about making some dramatic revelation at one of the higher profile conferences. Then he'd gone quiet and had withdrawn from everything. The papers weren't published, the conferences had passed and, with little fuss, he'd retired at the end of that academic year. Graham had been hopping between a series of sites around the Mediterranean at the time, part of a collaboration with a team from Athens University and had only been able to follow the events intermittently.

With the aid of another glass of scotch, he put the finishing touches to the speech, checked it over and then went up to his room and bed.

Funerals are never nice, people say they are nice, or the service lovely, but funerals are mostly just uncomfortable. Nobody quite knows what to do, and everyone is excruciatingly conscious about what they say. Graham had no idea who else might be there or if the professor even had any relatives. He'd been retired for the best part of a decade. How many of his old University associates would still be around, could still be bothered to show up? That Graham had been asked to do the eulogy indicated there was no one closer prepared to do the honours.

The service was being held at the city crematorium. The professor hadn't been a religious man, though he'd admitted, on occasion, that he found the idea of ritual rather comforting. After Graham had crunched the land rover to a halt on the gravel of the car park, he reclaimed his speech notes from the passenger seat and gave them another scan. His lips moved slightly as he practised his delivery. Satisfied with the words he'd chosen, he pocketed the notes, locked the car and crossed to the front of the building. The sun, in a more protracted performance today, was dodging benign cumulus clouds and making an effort at warmth that hinted of the coming summer. Across the surrounding memorial gardens, bright colours marked the plaques of loved ones where flowers had been left. A knot of mourners had gathered on the paving that edged the building. More of a turnout than he'd expected. Graham spotted some old acquaintances from the Exeter archaeology department and greeted them with the usual inconsequential exchanges of people who had little real interest in one another's affairs, but felt a comfort, at such times, in having known each other.

"Chandlers, you dumb shit, glad you could make it."

Graham hardly had time to turn before he was taken in a beardy, back-pounding embrace.

"Tinkerbell, good to see you," said Graham, muffled in the musky, cable-knit folds of the man's jumper. "I think you may have crushed my spine."

Dr Timothy Bell–Tinkerbell to friends and anyone who would drink with him–had arrived at Exeter to study for his doctorate in the same year Graham had begun his own. They'd never been rivals academically: Graham preferring his symbols and translations, where Tinkerbell had liked digging holes. But there had always been as much friction between them as comradely affection.

Graham was released from the ursine hug.

"It's a rum thing you had to come down for this." Tinkerbell's gesture took in the crematorium and the assembled mourners.

"Well, I could hardly not come. If it wasn't for the professor, I'd probably be working as a guide in a museum or something. Besides, the lady who rang asked me to do the eulogy."

"Lady? Oh, you mean the daughter." Tinkerbell gave a dismissive shrug. "So, you coming to the wake after? We're all going down to the Imperial to drain a few barrels in memory of the old sod, if you fancy stepping down from your lofty Cambridge cloud and joining us Devonian mud slingers."

"As long as you don't start any fights."

"I'm offended. I never start fights. It's always the other guys, they pick on me."

Graham heard his name and turned to see an attractive, dark-haired woman wave to him from beside the entrance to the chapel.

"That's the one, his daughter. Bit of an odd peg if you ask me," said Tinkerbell, in a loud whisper.

"Better say hello then, hadn't I. I'll catch you afterwards," Graham said, patting his old friend on the shoulder before walking over to where the woman was standing.

"Hello, Dr Chandlers, I'm Rosetta. We spoke on the telephone last week. I've seen your picture, but I wasn't sure."

It was the same rough silk voice, the same unplaceable accent. The speaker was younger than Graham had expected, perhaps early twenties, though she leant stiffly on a walking stick as she stepped forward to greet him. She was also one of the most naturally beautiful women he'd ever encountered, with honey tinted skin, underlain by a delicate, yet well-defined bone structure. She studied him with large, dark eyes, eyes framed by almost indecently long lashes, while her curved lips formed a smile as charming and mysterious as her accent. Caught as he was in that gaze, he was surprised when he felt the odd curl and fragile grip of the hand she put in his. He had a momentary fear that, if he squeezed, he might turn the bones in her hand to fragments. Truly, she was an unusual individual but in a way that intrigued.

"I'm sorry about the professor... your father, he was a good man."

She glanced through the open doors of the crematorium, a far off expression crossing her features.

"Yes, he was. It's going to be hard facing the world without him."

Graham knew the professor had been married, but his wife had been older and had died after a long battle with cancer some fifteen years ago. This woman seemed just too young –as well as having a hint of the Near East about her– to be the result of that marriage. Before they could talk further, a man in a formal, dark suit stepped out through the crematorium doors and asked the assembled mourners to enter and take their seats for the service. Classical music, played softly as the crowd shuffled their way inside the modern chapel and seated themselves. At the front was a simple casket of pale unvarnished wood. To one side stood a lectern and, after an all too brief opening by the man from the crematorium, it was to this that Graham was called. Taking the notes from his pocket, Graham barely glanced at them before beginning the eulogy. He covered a little about the professor's upbringing, extolled his academic deeds and touched upon the love for his wife and the selfless care he gave during her long illness. Switching back to his archaeological work, Graham raised a few chuckles from the people present when he related the incident when Alan, then only Dr Hargreaves, had been digging an important site in Tunis. They'd arrived one morning to find workmen had ruptured a pipe further up the hill and the entire, meticulously worked, excavation had been filled to a depth of two feet with raw sewage.

He talked a little more about the professor's influence on the world of archaeology and on himself in particular, and that the man would be missed by everyone who knew him. Then, looking up and seeing her sitting by herself in the front row Graham added: "and he will be particularly missed by his daughter."

He coughed, and folded the sheet of notes as another classical music track swelled from the hidden sound system. Stepping down from the lectern, he took a seat in the second row. After a contemplative pause, the man from the crematorium came forward once more.

"Now, before his body passes through the curtain to be cremated, Alan's daughter, Rosetta, will perform the alternative funeral rights in accordance with his wishes."

Graham looked up, surprised to see she had slipped off her coat to reveal she was wearing a short, rust-coloured dress cinched at the waist by a woven knot-work belt of the same hue. It revealed her legs and slender figure in a way that seemed shockingly inappropriate for a funeral service. She stepped with stiff movements to the space in front of the coffin and was carefully handed two clay cups by the man from the crematorium. Holding the cups aloft she began chanting in husky melodious tones. Graham didn't regard himself, in any real sense, a Christian, but a very British part of him was slightly appalled by the display –while another part was fascinated. Having offered the cups to the four quarters, Rosetta now stood at the foot of the coffin, her back to the room, and began a long recitation in a foreign language. Definitely an Indo-European tongue. It took him a while to realise he could follow much of what she was saying. It took a further thrill of realisation that she was saying it in the language of the ancient Hittites. She was speaking slowly, almost chanting, but he struggled to keep up with a translation.

"...the thirty-two who are named and the thirty-two who should not be named, the dark places below the land to be taken. And judged not and punished not he shall be, for by the deeds of his life a worthy man he is proved."

Her pronunciation was a bit peculiar, though she must have practised, as the delivery was almost oratorical.

"Oil, I give you," Rosetta said, as she cast the viscous contents of the first cup over the coffin lid. "That hunger will not afflict you, that your skin be cleansed, and that light you shall have. Rich and sweet spices I give you," she said, casting the powdered contents of the second cup in a dark fan across the oily surface and filling the room with the scent of cinnamon and juniper. "That the

14

rich taste of life and the sweetness of those who love you will always be in your memories."

She gave a low moan and embraced the casket, pressing her face into the mess on top. "The acolytes will now take you, that your flesh will be turned to flame, that your journey may begin."

Rosetta then stood straight, holding her hands out from her sides and nodded once to the crematorium man. She remained standing as the music started up, the curtains at the back flowed smoothly apart and whatever mechanism there was, rolled the coffin through. Once the curtains had closed, she turned and hobbled towards the seat where she'd left her coat and walking stick. Graham got up and hurried over as the other mourners began filing out, some looking bemused, others glancing in her direction with disapproval. Tinkerbell twirled his finger beside his ear and raised his thick eyebrows. Graham ignored him and moved to help Rosetta put on her coat. He waited as her underpowered fingers worked the buttons through the holes, before offering her his handkerchief –thanking provenance he'd thought to bring a clean one.

"Thanks," she said, dabbing at her eyes.

"Um, you've got oil and other stuff on your face."

"Yes, sorry, of course. I must seem foolish to you," she said, wiping her cheek.

"No, not at all. It was just, well, not what I would have expected," he said, watching the last of the other mourners as they passed through the doors. "Though, there was nothing wrong with it. Hattic, very, erm... fitting," he added, wincing internally at the clumsiness of his words. "Would you like a lift to the wake?"

"Thanks, but no. It'll all be academic people. I'm

just going to go home. The funeral car is taking me." She handed the handkerchief back. "Thank you for the words you said about my father, he would have appreciated them."

"It was the least I could do for him," Graham said, gesturing for her to precede him out of the chapel. "Your speech was really well delivered. Unusual. Though I expect I was the only one present who had a hope of understanding what you were saying."

She glanced over her shoulder "Thank you," she said. "That means a lot to me."

As they emerged into the bright sunshine, the black car was already waiting. So was Tinkerbell.

"Thought you might need someone to help you find your way to the wake, Dr C," he said, pointing first to his rear then his elbow.

"You needed a lift then?" said Graham.

"I passed up the opportunity to be first at the bar to wait for you. That's how much I value your company and your dubious academic opinions." Tinkerbell smiled, then winked at Rosetta and pulled the car door open for her.

"It's like being herded by the irresistible force," said Graham. "I'm really sorry about your father and I'm sorry you and I didn't get a chance to meet before... Well, under better circumstances."

Rosetta turned to Graham and put her delicate hand upon his.

"I'm also sorry, but I am pleased to have finally met you. Do you need to get back to Cambridge this evening, or are you staying longer?" she said, looking into his eyes. It wasn't a pass, he knew it couldn't be a pass, but part of him leapt at the thought.

"I'm booked into the Rougemont for a couple of nights. I thought I might visit a few old haunts while I'm here."

"You going to drop in to the department and say hi to everyone?" said Tinkerbell.

"Maybe."

"If you have time, Dr Chandlers, would you mind coming by the house?" said Rosetta. "There's a few things my father wanted you to have –books and notes and similar. I could offer you some lunch, if it wouldn't be too much of an imposition?"

"Please, call me Graham. I can't see how you could be an imposition on anybody. I'd love to come."

Can't see how you could be an imposition on anybody –he could have kicked himself. The poor girl was still grieving for her father and he was flirting with her.

"Ah, that's really handy, the professor wanted me to pick up one of his old journals. If I could cadge a lift as well," said Tinkerbell.

Graham swallowed an unhealthy twinge of annoyance at his old friend.

"That's fine. I'll make lunch for both of you. Until tomorrow, Dr Bell, Dr Chandlers... sorry, Graham." She climbed into the car and Tinkerbell shut the door after her, giving a small wave as the car pulled away.

"Come on Tink," said Graham, heading towards his own vehicle. "I'm sure there's plenty of ale left."

2: Exeter

Graham's alarm went off at the usual time the following morning but, after trying out consciousness, he decided it wasn't a good idea and slept late. Predictably, the wake had started out as a gathering of friends and associates recalling their memories of the professor's life, proceeding through to a group of academics earnestly discussing their own or each others' work, and finally on to a table full of beered-up blokes loudly talking a load of crap. The evening had come to an end after Tinkerbell was politely told he'd had enough to drink by the bar staff and had subsequently tried to take a swing at one of the bouncers.

By the time Graham finally got himself out of bed, the hotel had stopped serving breakfast. Not that he minded, given the instability of his innards. He'd told Tinkerbell he'd meet him at half-twelve in the hotel foyer. So, with nothing in particular to do for a couple of hours he walked into the town-centre, past the cathedral and maze-like shopping precincts, until he found the cobbled street leading up to the castle. The cafe was still there, though he didn't recognise any of the staff. He'd worked there as an undergraduate, and then continued to frequent the place even after he'd started earning money during his doctorate. He still couldn't face food, but the walk had helped enough that coffee seemed like a good idea. He nursed it while he read a newspaper a previous customer had left behind. After a while he ended up staring out of the window, looking at the pink, weathered stone of the castle walls visible beyond. This woman he was seeing today, a woman with restricted use of her hands, who walked with a stick, how had she come into the professor's life? Who had taught her to form word sounds in the language of the Hittites like that? The professor knew the various cuneiform texts and languages, but he was no palaeo-linguist.

With midday past, Graham returned to the hotel. Tinkerbell rose from one of the sofas as Graham stepped into the reception area. He appeared to be wearing the same clothing he'd had on the previous evening.

"Nice black-eye, Dr Bell."

"Badge of honour, Dr Chandlers. Mark of a good night out. So, how's your head this morning? You fit to drive?"

Graham nodded and led him to where the Discovery was parked.

"Did I tell you about that undisturbed cist burial we excavated on Dartmoor last year?" said Tinkerbell, as they climbed in.

"Yes, you told me last night," said Graham, putting the key in the ignition and starting the engine.

Tinkerbell sniffed and scratched at his beard "Oh, yeah. Course I did."

They drove Northwards into the more genteel side of Exeter, past the University and on into the surrounding leafy suburbs.

"So, the professor's daughter. How come I've never even known he had one?" asked Graham, as he turned the car onto the Cowley Bridge spanning the red tinted waters of the River Exe.

"After your time, Dr C. Just after the whole debacle in Samuha with that dig which went tits-up. He'd found some orphaned cripple while he was working out there. Had her adopted so he could bring her back and care for her here. This was still on University time, you have to understand. He'd used up all his leave, so he took an unpaid sabbatical. Course when he came back to work, he wasn't really the same. He was never going to get another permit to dig from the Turkish Authorities and the papers he started writing were, let's say, a little off the accepted track. At his age, I just don't think he was up to caring for a disabled child and juggling an academic career at the same time. I guess that's why he retired."

The professor's house was in Brampford Speke, a cosy village beside the River, a mere twenty minute drive from the University. Graham could remember the way as he came to each landmark, but Tinkerbell insisted on directing him anyway. The fine old Victorian mansion had changed little since Graham had last seen it, easily more than a decade ago. Rosetta opened the door before he even had a chance to touch the doorbell. Inviting them in, she showed them through to a comfortable looking parlour at the back of the house, where a lithe, coffee coloured cat regarded them with a mistrustful gaze from the back of the sofa. There was a stillness to the place that was both restful and lonely.

Rosetta had prepared a lunch of quiche with salad and new potatoes. They ate, sat at a table by the double sash windows which gave a view over the garden and the green and red patchwork of the Exe Valley beyond. They talked of inconsequential things at first, the weather, the landscape, Tink's black eye, then she attempted to tell them about the sense-robbing shock of seeing the man who had become her father collapse in the hall after a simple trip to the shop to buy milk and bread. Graham felt her glancing at him more than Tinkerbell.

"Sorry," she said, lowering her dark eyes, putting her hand to her mouth and taking several shuddering breaths. He should have reached across the table and taken her hand, offered her the comfort she so clearly needed, but it didn't seem right with Tinkerbell there. He didn't trust his own motives either. Ashamed, he let the moment hang. Rosetta dabbed at her eyes with the back of her hand then, mumbling another apology, she stood and began gathering the plates, putting them on the tray she'd brought it all in on.

"Here, let me," said Graham, getting up and taking the tray.

Her lips tugged into a smile and she indicated the way to the kitchen. "Please, just put it on the work-top there. I'll deal with it all in a minute," she said, turning as Tinkerbell appeared at the doorway. "I suppose I'd better show you his office."

Rosetta took them out to the hallway and ascended the grand staircase with deliberate care. It occupied a broad and airy space, splashed with colour from a generous picture window where the stairway turned back on itself. At the top, she led them down a short corridor and opened a door halfway along. The study was modestly proportioned, with a small Edwardian desk, a wooden chair under the window and a worn and misshapen leather sofa against the opposite wall. A workbench turned-display-shelf spanned the longer wall, supporting a variety of pottery and other artefacts, including a complete, and heavy looking, granite quern as well as an open box containing what appeared to be a number of darkened bones from a human foot. The remaining walls were lined with shelves stuffed with books, box files, old periodicals and field notes. Several empty boxes had been set out on the sofa.

"He'd requested that you should take all his notes and journals, but the books and magazines are no use to me either, so you might as well take them too." Rosetta moved over to the workbench and touched a piece of twisted and parched leather which had probably once been the sole of a sandal. "All of these as well. I've had enough of ancient things."

"I can take the journals and such, but I'll never be able to manage all the other stuff, it won't all fit in the car," said Graham. He looked at Tinkerbell. "Would the Exeter department take some?"

Tinkerbell regarded the shelves with a critical eye. "The periodicals could probably find a home. I dare say some of the books too. Damned if we need anymore tut cluttering up the place, though." He gestured to the arte-facts. "We could generously donate it to the chumps at the museum?"

"Yes, good call. Though, those boxes are never going to fit it all. How about if we pack up the things for the university and museum first. I can run you back into Exeter and pick up some more boxes while I'm there," said Graham.

"I'll leave you gentlemen to it. Coffee for both?" said Rosetta.

After their affirmations, she went back downstairs.

"Best get started, then," said Tinkerbell, pulling out a box file and leafing through its contents. "Mind, if I take this? It's got some notes that could be relevant to my research."

"Go ahead, the more you take, the less I have to." Graham glanced around. "I'll start on the books. Why don't you see if Rosetta's got any old newspapers for packing up these artefacts?"

"There's no need, Grandpa, we have all the modern packing materials we need in here," said Tinkerbell, fishing bubble-wrap and a roll of parcel tape out of one of the boxes.

They packed for an hour, before Tinkerbell stood and rolled his neck like a prize-fighter. "Time for more coffee, I think. If our hostess will provide. You?"

Graham nodded and continued packing while Tinkerbell thumped down the stairs in search of Rosetta. Minutes later he returned holding an eighteen-inch shard of pot with an unusual pearlescent glaze on one side. He reached for a fresh piece of bubble-wrap.

"Where'd you get that Tink?"

"Staircase. Window ledge. You walked right past it on the way up."

"I don't know if she meant for us to take everything in the house. Let me see?"

"There's no point in her keeping it, it's obviously a fake," Tinkerbell said, handing it over.

It was from the upper part of what must have been a very large earthenware storage vessel. On the outside the pot looked authentic enough, old, very old. The seed twist pattern running around it was done with enough care that the vessel would have been of importance, perhaps a village store of oil, or something ceremonial. On the inner surface it was a different story; the glaze was like the inside of an abalone shell, mostly silver-white with hints of blue-green where the surface appeared to turn in lazy coils. It was beautiful, but certainly not appropriate to the period the outside suggested. Through one corner was a tiny drill hole.

"Not that!"

Graham hadn't seen Rosetta enter the room. She tossed the tray she was holding onto the desk, slopping coffee across it in her haste, and lunged towards him.

"Whoa! Steady," he said.

"It's," she produced an unintelligible word which sounded like ittraem, "you can't take it." Rosetta grabbed the shard from Graham, but her ineffectual hands failed to hold the awkward shape properly and it slipped. Graham's reactions were instinctive and he caught it before the fragile ceramic hit the floor. He lifted it and pushed the shard into her hands until he knew she had it gripped. Rosetta let out a guttural moan and, clutching it to her chest, she lurched from the room. A couple of moments later a door slammed somewhere along the corridor. Graham exchanged a glance with Tinkerbell, then started to follow, but Tinkerbell shook his head. In silence they went back to packing, disturbed by the occasional muffled sob through the walls.

Once the boxes had been filled, Tinkerbell and Graham carried them out to the Discovery and loaded them in the back. Tinkerbell stayed down by the car to call a friend at the museum on his mobile. Graham went back upstairs and gently tapped on the door to Rosetta's room.

"Rosetta, we're going to take the things off to the museum now." He waited a moment, then turned to go.

The door opened behind him and Graham looked back. Rosetta was standing in the doorway, her red

25

rimmed eyes downcast.

"I'm sorry," she said, sniffing. "You must think I'm being ridiculous."

"No, not at all," said Graham. Her behaviour had been somewhat over-dramatic, but she had just lost her father. "There's no point in bottling it up. You're grieving, it's something you need to go through."

She gave him a tight smile and nodded. "Have you got everything?" she said, walking down the corridor and looking into the study.

"There's still the books, journals and other notes. There aren't enough boxes, and there isn't enough room in the back of my car, for that matter."

"Oh, but those are the things my father wanted you to take. You are going to come back for them aren't you?"

He'd briefly considered trying to drive back to Cambridge that afternoon. It would have been a late evening arrival, but at least he'd have been able to get back to work tomorrow. He gave up the notion. He owed enough to the professor that he'd stay another night to help his daughter out.

"I need to get some more boxes sorted out, but I'll try."

"Oh, do. I'll make you something for dinner?" She gave a rueful smile. "I'm not actually much of a cook, though I can manage pretty well between the freezer and the microwave."

Graham smiled back. "When you put it like that, how can I refuse?"

"Thanks. Don't worry about the time, I'll start dinner when you get here."

"Right, I'll be off then." Not knowing how to take his leave, Graham felt the pause lengthening into awkward-ness.

Rosetta leant forward and kissed him on the cheek. "Go. I'll be fine."

The feel of that contact lingered as he left the house and drove with Tinkerbell back to Exeter. Yes, he was sexually attracted to her, but he was experienced and mature enough to know it was likely to lead to heartache or embarrassment. But there was something...

"You don't want to go this way, dipstick." Tinkerbell said, looking over his shoulder at the junction they had just passed. "Just double back at the next roundabout and then left at the one we've just crossed."

"Oh, sorry. Yes, I'm being stupid."

Following Tinkerbell's directions, they made it to the museum without any further detours. The place had been completely refurbished since he'd last seen it. The assistant curator who met them, one of Tinkerbell's graduate students, showed Graham around the newly added buildings. He admitted the director would probably be less than pleased about accepting boxes of random and unspecified finds, though he was looking forward to having a look himself. He also offered to give Graham as many cartons as he needed; they still had hundreds left from moving all the archives during the renovations. With that duty dispensed, Tinkerbell took his leave and headed back to the university. He declined a lift, claiming the fifteen minute walk would burn off some of the calories he'd imbibed the previous evening. He'd probably need a fifteen mile walk to make any serious impact.

Graham arrived back at the house in Brampford Speke in the late afternoon. He didn't really know what to expect. Rosetta took longer to answer the door, but then she wasn't expecting him to arrive at any particular time.

"Is that going to be enough?" she asked, as Graham brought the first couple of boxes from the back of the car and stacked them in the hallway.

"We'll see," he said.

In the end they filled five.

"Oops," said Graham, putting a hand to his forehead and glancing around the study.

"What is it?" A look of concern drawing her eyebrows together.

"Have you got some more parcel tape? I must have put the roll in with the stuff we took to the museum." She opened the desk and hooked out a new roll. "Here, if I hold the lid shut could you stick it down?" "There's a lot of things I can do, and a some I can't," she said, holding it out. "I'm afraid sticky tape is not on my list of easy. Though it's a marvelous invention. I just don't have the fine control or strength."

"Oh crap, sorry, I forgot. How long have you...?" Graham said, taking the roll of tape and gesturing towards her hands.

The moment she considered turned into a few seconds.

"Let's say, somewhat over ten years."

"Sorry, I didn't mean to pry."

"No, it's not that I mind you asking. It's just a bit difficult to explain to people. To put it in simple terms, I had something like a life-changing experience as child and ended up with various complications. As a result some of the bones in my joints became fused and the tendons shortened. I had to have a number of operations over several years. My father was wonderful, he got me the best medical care, but I was in a wheelchair until I was sixteen. Even now, I still see a physiotherapist every few months. Though I can do pretty much everything for myself, even parcel tape given enough time and effort."

Graham smiled and pulled out a length of tape. "But it's easier if you have a tactless idiot available to do it for you."

She returned his smile and bent to hold the flaps of the box down while he taped. Once they were done and with all the boxes packed the room had a sad and bare look to it.

"I was thinking of having a space where I could meditate and do yoga. Though I may keep it as a study," said Rosetta in response to Graham's unasked question. She looked towards the window. "It's such a big world. So many parts to it, so many people. I still don't really know what I'm going to be doing with my life." She shrugged and looked back at Graham. "First things first, I need to be making something for dinner."

He chuckled and gestured for her to precede him. She made her way downstairs to begin her preparations in the kitchen. Graham followed her, carrying the first of the boxes out to the car. As he came back up the stairs for the next, he noted the empty stand on the windowsill, the shard had not been put back on display.

The meal she prepared was not so dissimilar to the sort of thing he'd have made for her if she'd been visiting his flat: fresh-made pasta from a packet with a sauce from a jar. The bottle of wine she produced, however, was a Margaux, undoubtedly as good as anything the sommelier at the main hall of Corpus Christi might come up with. She solemnly handed him a corkscrew.

Graham raised an eyebrow. "Are you sure? That's an expensive bottle of wine and once it's opened... I shouldn't have much. I've got to drive back to the hotel."

"It's fine. A fitting tribute to my father. I'm only sorry he didn't have a chance to drink it himself. But you can stay if you want? The bed in the spare room is all made up."

And now she was asking him to stay the night. He still didn't know how to read her. He'd just have to take it slow, but she had depths to explore beyond her obvious youth and beauty.

"Thanks, I'd like that," he said, taking the bottle and doing the honours with the cork.

They sat down for their meal at the oak kitchen table, relishing the vintage Bordeaux with its subtle aromas and complex flavours. Graham asked her about her real parents, and where she had been born.

"I'm from the central area of Turkey. My parents gave me up when I was little. They didn't reject me or anything, but they sent me to serve at... at something like a religious school. I still got to see them occasionally."

Graham nodded. "You never tempted to try to get back in touch with them?"

"Oh, they're dead now. I would have if they were still alive. It isn't like I bore them any ill-will."

"I'm sorry."

"It's fine, it was a long time ago. The professor is... was the only family I've had since." The look that crossed her features spoke of a deep sadness, kept at bay for another time. Graham changed tack.

"The words you spoke at the funeral service, it took me a while to catch on to what you were saying. It seemed a bit outlandish at the time, but in hindsight it was entirely fitting for the professor. A ritual to mark the occasion. Something to shake up the old fuddy-duddies." He smiled to show there was no criticism. "That was pretty good Hattic," he added. "Better than any of the students I teach. Frankly, better than most of the academics I know. I'm intrigued. Did you learn that speech as a one off, or do you actually understand the language?"

Rosetta looked at him under lowered lashes. "It's a simpler language than English."

"Can you read it as well? In cuneiform?"

She smiled.

"Good God, I can get you a place in my department straight-off with those kind of skills. Where did you study? Was it here in Exeter?" He regarded her as she slowly shook her head. "Was this all from the professor? I know he was a good teacher, but the intricacies of language itself weren't in his field."

"The professor helped me, but he found a better way."

"What? How?"

In answer, she got up and walked over to the carved oak sideboard occupying one wall. Opening a pair of cupboard doors she revealed a stereo system. She reached in and fiddled for a few moments getting an old-fashioned tape cassette from its box, pressing a couple of buttons and putting it into the player. A moment later, Graham's own voice came over the speakers saying the words "the man is in the house," then repeating the same phrase translated in Hattic. The recording went on to break the phrase down into the individual words and restructure it using different nouns: the woman is in the house, the man is in the water and so on.

"I've known your voice for many years now," she said.

"So you learnt to speak Hattic from those old tapes?"

"In a manner of speaking." she said, her lips curving. "How old were you?"

She sighed "About twelve or so. I found your voice comforting. It's funny but, when I first spoke to you last week on the telephone, it was like I already knew you."

"I'd forgotten the professor even had those tapes. It was years ago, some concept of teaching ancient languages in the same way we teach modern languages with tapes. At least, I think that was what he wanted. It never came to anything." Graham listened to the tape a bit more. "You know, some of my old ideas about pronunciation are outdated now."

He hadn't heard her properly laugh before, an almost silent, throaty laugh that went on for a minute or two.

"What?"

"Outdated... Sorry, I shouldn't laugh," she said, catching her breath and covering her eyes with her hand.

"Hey, it's okay."

She lifted her head and looked him in the eye "So, what did you think of my pronunciation? Is that outdated too?"

"It was certainly pretty stilted. Interesting idea to chant the words."

"That particular ceremony is supposed to be chanted."

"I know most of what's stored here in Exeter, as well much of the published transcriptions: It's not a piece I recall coming across. Do you know where the original clay came from?"

"It's not from a clay, those words were too sacred to be written down. They were passed on by word of mouth."

Graham made a disparaging noise. She was clearly

an intelligent woman, and he'd hoped to have had a conversation with her on an academic level, but this was headed away from fact into the realms of make-believe. "So you just skipped back three thousand years and picked up a few tips on funeral ceremonies from a handy Hittite priest?"

Her lips formed that mysterious smile again. "Those tapes." She cocked her head to listen to his voice still pronouncing words in Hattic in the background. "I learned English from them, not the other way round."

Graham raised his eyebrow. "What are you saying? That there's a pocket of native Hattic speakers who have somehow survived in an isolated part of the Turkish mountains? I'd like to see that. Even so, the language ought to have altered over time, it's inevitable. Like the difference between modern and ancient Greek or middle and modern English. The language spoken by the ancient Hittites would be almost unrecognisable to a contemporary speaker."

"You managed to understand the words I spoke."
"Yes, well, you had the tapes to pick it up from."

"I told you, Nesli is my native language." She used the name for Hattic the Hittites would have used. "Rituals, as well as the written form, were more formal. You'd be the one who probably wouldn't recognise the spoken form. It was spoken more rapidly, and the speakers would often make their phrasing more musical or rhythmic at the expense of syntax."

"Oh, right," he said. Putting his hand up and shaking it. It wasn't like him to get riled by a good academic debate on the nature of language. But then this wasn't academic. He'd done Hattic, moved on to other things. He was at the top of his field. There were few enough people in the world who could even read it, let alone attempt to follow the nuances of a spoken form, but here was this girl, hardly older than some of his third year undergraduates, telling him he was quite mistaken about much of his groundwork understanding of the ancient language.

She looked at him seriously. "What if someone who was there at the time had been able to arrive here in the twenty-first century, their knowledge and experiences intact?"

"Sorry, I thought we were talking about science here, not science-fiction. I mean yes, we work on a lot of conjecture and hunches, but we then apply the scientific method to seek to prove, or at least back up a hypothesis. Ideas about time travel or being visited by ancient beings is a quick route to being discredited in archaeological circles. Like there aren't enough nutters and conspiracy theorists around." He stood up. "Look, it's getting late, I should go."

"But there's so much I wanted to talk to you about. Please, can you stay?"

An attractive young woman suggesting he stay the night was not something to pass up under normal circumstances, even if the message was not yet clear and rational concern warred briefly with primaeval desire but, for once, won.

"Thanks, but I'd better get back to my hotel. I've got to head off early tomorrow," he said. Much as she'd wound him up, he'd feel terrible even attempting to take advantage of a young woman who was grieving for her dead parent. He'd feel even more terrible if the long sad looks she was giving him, just meant she would be glad of the company, and not the sexual advances of a man ten years her senior.

He left the house, got into the Discovery and started the engine. Glancing back once at the disconsolate figure framed in the doorway, he sighed, put the car in gear and pulled away.

3: Cambridge

The work he'd put off for the trip to Exeter hadn't gone away, it had accumulated. He still had that paper to finish writing, but now a box-full of clays had arrived from Jordan and a dozen student essays were waiting on his desk ready for marking. He opened the box and carefully unwrapped one of the clay tablets. It was badly worn and the marks which had been pressed into its surface barely legible. Getting any meaningful translation was going to be hard work. He brought it to the window where the light was better but, instead of looking at the writing of someone long dead, he watched the students crossing the quad below, meeting and chatting. Should he have left Rosetta like that? Maybe she was a crackpot and needy, but she wasn't demanding. And there was something about her, not simply her looks, but some indefinable quality that fascinated him. He turned back to his desk, placed the tablet in its foam cocoon and put his hand on the phone. Would it be a good idea to call her, just to check she was okay? He took his hand away and picked up the tablet again. He didn't need any more complications right now.

The reminder he'd brought back from Exeter,

however, was still there when he got home. Every time Graham tried to cross his living room. He cursed Rosetta roundly when, negotiating the obstacle course of heavy boxes with his dinner plate in hand, he managed to slop pasta sauce onto the carpet. He put the dish down on the coffee table and went to fetch a cloth. It was ridiculous blaming her anyway. If it was anyone's fault it was Professor Hargreaves's, firstly for having a weak blood vessel in his head and, secondly, for believing Graham would have any interest in all his accumulated writings. He finished wiping the carpet; it didn't look like it had stained. Mid-brown had been a good choice, if a dull one. Putting the cloth back in the kitchen and retrieving his dinner, he sat down on the sofa and looked over the clutter; a lifetime's work reduced to a mere five boxes. Perhaps five was good, some people may not even fill one.

He took a forkful of food without paying much attention to what he was eating. The best thing to do would be to just get on with it, go through it all methodically and throw out anything that was rubbish. He picked up the knife he'd brought through with his plate. Using a few deft strokes he slit open the top of the nearest box and examined the contents as he ate.

By the time he'd finished his meal he had discovered a number of what appeared to be fictional stories of ancient Gods and heroes, even a number of sheets of what looked like verse, though it didn't rhyme. There were also a great many notes for early papers the professor had written. Graham was interested to learn more about the mysterious and unpublished papers the man had been working on before he retired and skimmed through the contents without finding anything of relevance. He opened the next box and found the professor's field journals, relating to each of his digs. Graham picked up the topmost –Samuha, Turkey: Summer 2002 written on its cover. That problematic last dig the professor had undertaken. He leafed through the first few pages. It concerned the team's arrival in Turkey and preparations for the dig. It seemed that, at the time, the Turkish authorities had become very concerned about ancient artefacts being taken abroad; claiming, probably quite rightly, that it was a drain on the nation's venerable cultural heritage. Unfortunately for the professor, it had added extra layers of bureaucratic complexity to their project and getting a licence to dig had come with a number of conditions attached.

The team was small: just the professor, Gail Scott, acting as assistant, and two postgraduate students: Sam Heaver and Chris Tucker. But having a small team allowed the dig, on a modest budget, to last most of the summer. Graham had known Gail Scott at Exeter, she knew her stuff. She'd since moved on to a high-flying administrative post at the British Museum. The two postgrads, he wasn't familiar with.

Graham put the journal to one side and opened the other three boxes, still seeking anything about the mysterious papers. The best he could come up with was a folder containing a few hand-written notes waxing strong about a discovery that offered a complete and contextual understanding of the languages of ancient Anatolia. The folder also contained a printed sheet with the date: 14/12/2002 at the top and page 2 at the bottom. The sheet detailed issues concerning the age of a large fragment of unusually glazed pottery, but gave no reference to which fragment, or who had written the report.

Whatever it had been stapled to, was now lost. Was it referring to the shard at the professor's house? The shard Rosetta had been so possessive about? The date was about right for when the professor would have been putting together the material for the mystery papers.

Graham picked up his mobile and scrolled through to the professor's... no, Rosetta's number and hit dial. It rang for a long time with no answer. Odd that she wouldn't be there, but then he knew very little about her habits.

The following morning Graham dutifully got on with the translations on the clays he'd been given. At ten thirty, he left to oversee his seminar group for that term —one of the faculty obligations for his post. They had been discussing how the general record of ancient written material could only offer a tiny window on what had occurred in history.

One of the students raised her hand. "Dr Chandlers, how is it possible to accurately date the writing on a scroll or tablet, if the date isn't written on it?"

"A pertinent question, Liwei," he replied. "Dating accuracy is an interesting field. Anyone got any ideas about how we might go about that?"

Gareth, one of the other students sat forward. "Sometimes the age of other finds in the same strata of a dig might help date a tablet," he said.

Another student, Helena added. "A lot of dating can be done by cross referencing the content. Many cultures referred to events or Kings from other places, the dates for which are already known."

"Good. It also works in reverse. We can use this to help date strata in dig sites by that kind of cross refer- encing of any tablets or papyri found. Of course, these days, we can also have items sent to be tested in the laboratory using carbon dating for hide or papyrus, or in the case of clay..."

He opened his jotter and made a note in the corner. Clay, yes, or pottery, the report in the professor's folder could well have been from a lab.

"Dr Chandlers?"

"Oh sorry. Yes, in the case of clay tablets we would send it to be tested by thermoluminescence."

The seminar wound up at twelve and Graham headed back to his office. After flicking through his address book, he picked up the phone and dialled. It rang three times before being answered.

"What's the secret password?" said the person on the other end of the line.

"Tinkerbell, is that you?" said Graham.

"What's the password?

"You're a knob, you know that don't you?"

"Correct. How can I help you, Dr C?"

"This is a bit of a long shot, but you remember that big shard of pottery up at the professor's place? The one with the mother of pearl glazing inside? It had a drill hole on it. I was wondering if the professor ever submitted it for testing through your department down in Exeter?"

"What? That bauble the girl was all sentimental about? Come on Dr C, you know as well as I do that piece of tut's a fake. At best, someone's got hold of a chunk of genuine pot and painted that shiny stuff on the inside. Fooling thermoluminescence using old material is pretty easy. You know, it's big business in the Middle East.

"So he didn't have it tested then?"

"How the bloody hell should I know, it would have

been ten years ago?"

"Maybe I should talk to the Sub-Dean? See if there's a record?"

"He's pretty busy at the moment, with finals starting next week. To be honest, Graham, if the Prof had submitted that thing, I would actually have remembered. Everyone in the department would have remembered, and had a good laugh about it. I know you looked up to him, we all did, and we're all still upset about the old duffer popping his clogs, but it won't help by trying to make more of his past than there was. And I'm sorry the crazy cripple got to you."

"What? Do you mean Rosetta?"

"That whole sexy, mysterious allure thing she puts on. It's all for attention. She tries it on with anyone she meets. You can't blame her, having all those treatments, being stuck inside when all the other kids were out being teenagers. But she isn't just physically disabled, she's got herself some serious head issues. You saw her at the funeral. My advice there is just to smile and nod. Don't get drawn in."

Graham rang off. The logical part of his mind could see Tinkerbell was right. The other side, the irrational side, was annoyed at himself for thinking it –that side had already fallen for her hook, line and sinker. Still holding the phone, he looked up another number and punched it in.

"Oxford Thermoluminescence Lab, Jim Douglas speaking."

"Hello Jim, it's Graham Chandlers, have you got a moment? I was hoping you could help me track down a sample which might have been sent for testing from Exeter a few years ago."

"Sure, have you got a reference number?"

"No, but I've got a date, some time around 14th December 2002. It was a big piece, possibly from a site in Turkey. It had something that looked like mother-of-pearl glazing on the inner surface. It should be under Professor Hargreaves' name, if it isn't through the University."

"Okay, I'll check. Hold on while I look it up."

The phone was clunked down onto a hard surface. Graham could hear the sound of a keyboard getting a workout for a minute then Jim was back on the line.

"Sorry Graham, we've got no record of a test carried out on a piece like that. You sure it's been tested?"

"I haven't got it here, but someone had drilled a small hole in one corner. Which is usually an indication that a sample has been taken."

"Sounds like it. Still, it's not like we're the only lab. He could have even had it done abroad if he was paying for it himself. From the description, it would have been a fake anyway. Mother of pearl glaze, sort of thing the Victorians would have liked. Just as a thought –you know pearl nacre is half organic, have you checked the radiocarbon labs?"

"No, I hadn't even considered that."

Graham thanked Jim and rang off. Holding the phone crooked on his shoulder, he looked up the number for the radiocarbon labs and punched it in. The girl he normally dealt with had recently left and the guy he was put through to gave the impression he was much too busy to be looking up old files as favours. He took Graham's details anyway, and promised to get back to him.

Having wasted enough time on the matter, Graham spent the afternoon marking essays. That evening, after picking up a ready meal and a bottle of Rioja from Sainsbury's on the way home, he spent some time dividing the professor's papers into material worth keeping and things that could be thrown out. The journals should probably be kept for reference at the library, or even sent back to the archaeology department in Exeter. He put them to one side, then remembered the one he'd taken out. The one detailing the professor's final dig. Graham poured himself another glass of wine, sat down on the sofa, leafed through the journal and began reading from where he'd left off.

The first month's entries gave detailed accounts of the team's arrival at Ankara, along with the acquisition of supplies and extra equipment once there. To help with driving and various chores at the camp and dig site, they'd also hired a local man, Abbas –whom the professor had worked with previously, and described as a jocular fellow with muscles like walnuts and a lack of front teeth. The site itself, in a fairly remote region some four hours drive east of Ankara, was accessible by a dirt track through the hills.

The day after their arrival, having barely had time to set up their camp, less, look around the ruined city, the inspector appointed by the Turkish authorities had arrived. An archaeological bureaucrat from the museum in Ankara, clearly with an axe to grind about foreigners stealing all the glory and resentful that they were the ones who could get the funding. He seemed like he knew his stuff, though, and informed the professor that his team would not be allowed to dig at a number spots within the ancient site which had previously been identified as major buildings. After a token argument, the professor reluctantly conceded. He wasn't intending to dig on the main site anyway. The purpose of this project was to examine a smaller complex of ruins in the hills outside city confines, some quarter of a mile away. The inspector had informed them that he'd be back at the end of each week, to check their progress and ensure they were working within the terms of their licence.

The Professor and his team then spent the following few days lugging their equipment up the hill to the dig site and thoroughly surveying the complex. It had been a string of connected buildings. The remains of the thick walls followed the contours of the landscape on which they were built, much less uniform in shape than the city ruins in the valley below. At the end of the week they had identified several promising spots to put in exploratory trenches.

When the inspector had returned, he'd appeared pleased with the team's operations. He'd let the professor know he believed the complex to be a series of barns and farm buildings and, at best, that they may find a grain store. But the day after his visit, the inspector's theory was proved wrong when the first trench revealed shards of pottery and several clay tablets consistent with a building of high importance. A building that could possibly be, as the professor wrote, a religious centre for the whole region.

Graham sat back and poured himself another glass of wine. It seemed odd he hadn't heard more about this dig. Samuha was less known than some of the other sites of the ancient Hittite civilization He recalled some intriguing texts written about how the priests and kings had argued over temple and ceremonial rites, and how deities had been adopted from distant regions and brought to reside at the religious centre of the city. For the professor to have found that religious centre should have been major news in archaeological circles.

He picked up the journal again and read on. Not far from the outer wall of the biggest building, Sam had identified the corner of a large stone slab. Believing it may have been a decorative or carved stone from the building nearby, the professor allowed him to enlist the help of Abbas to excavate and lift it. What they discovered in doing so, was far more interesting. The slab was actually still in situ, one of a number of capstones from the ceiling of a partly back-filled conduit or passageway below. From the look, running from within the main building to somewhere below the hill behind.

This was, potentially, a very exciting discovery. The professor had instructed the others to continue their excavations within the building and attempt to discover where the passageway started –if it started in the building at all. He set Sam the task of carefully removing the fill from the bottom. After a further week, not only had Gail and Chris found a series of steps leading down to what must have been the start of the passageway, but Sam had managed to tunnel a further metre until he encountered another capstone, this one fallen inwards and effectively blocking the way. It took several days to dig it free and remove it but, having done so, they found the remaining two metres of the passageway ran almost unobstructed before opening into some kind of chamber.

The next entry in the journal detailed what would constitute every archaeologist's dream of discovery. Graham sat up straight, clutching the covers of the journal as he read it again.

June 12th 11.30am: Sam backed out of the passage

45

shaking with excitement. He informed me that there was a chamber at the other end, but wouldn't tell me what was in it, he just handed me the torch. I took it and crawled along the passage. After four metres the passageway opened out into a small chamber, some three metres square. The ceiling was higher, and I was able to stand without stooping to look around. I saw gods and tears of joy sprang to my eyes.

I was probably the first human being to enter this sacred space in millennia. It was a thought that made me giddy. The chamber might originally have been a natural cavern, but the walls had been carved in exquisite relief, depicting the various gods and goddesses of the Hittites. At the far side, a substantial alcove had been cut into the rock, some twenty centimetres above the current ground level. A large broken stone slab lay in front of this, part propped against the lip of the recess. It probably once sealed the front of the alcove and had fallen out at some point in its history. Yet more exciting was that within the niche, still intact and apparently in situ, sat a large earthenware vessel. It was of the kind typically used for the storage of grain or sometimes oil –though rarely found in such good condition. It had a heavy-feeling presence, in such a small space, that constantly drew the eye.

Any site with artefacts still in place was significant, but to be discovered in an undisturbed chamber, that was clearly of such religious significance, made it important. A major find. It seemed absurd that Graham had heard nothing about it, either from the professor or anyone else.

Graham read on, hungry to know more. As if on cue the inspector had arrived from Ankara the day after the chamber had been discovered. He'd insisted on going down for a look, even before Sam had finished setting up the light stands to allow them to work within the room. When the inspector emerged, he'd ordered the jar be brought to the museum in Ankara for proper examination. The professor had agreed in principle, whilst pointing out that both passageway and chamber had yet to be excavated down to the original floor level. He'd also pointed out that moving such a large and fragile vessel out through the narrow confines of the passageway, would prove difficult. The inspector had not been pleased, seeming to blame the professor for making it awkward to –as the professor put it in his journal– "get his sweaty palms on the loot." After taking a number of photographs, the inspector had left. He'd shown very little interest in the finds Gail and Chris had picked from their end of the dig.

They spent the next week excavating the floor, which had a layer of accumulation up to fourteen centimetres thick. They found a number of beads, that appeared to be from a necklace, and a couple of rather elegantly produced cuneiform tablets in the room. These were duly recorded in situ then removed to the camp for proper examination. They would have to be packaged up and sent to the University in Istanbul. From what they could tell from the tablets, they held in their neat impressions a number of previously unknown religious texts from the period. With most of the floor excavated, the three sections of slab that had covered the niche were then lifted and removed. On the underside –the side which would have faced the room– was a beautifully executed carving of one of the unnamed gods of the underworld, along with a smaller female figure who appeared to be his wife or perhaps a priestess.

The entry for the twentieth of June detailed bad news. The inspector had arrived in the morning, checked all their excavations and finds, and then informed them a team from the museum in Ankara would be arriving the next day to take over. He'd told them that permission to disturb the site any further was effectively revoked, and they were expected to hand over any materials and data from the excavation to the Ankara archaeologists. The professor took Gail and drove into the nearest town to make some phone calls and sort it out. They called Istanbul University, the museum in Ankara, even the ministry of Culture. In his journal, the professor described it as a totally unprofessional theft of another academic's work. Graham had to agree. He was surprised there hadn't been more of a stink about it afterwards. Why didn't Exeter University or the Archaeological society kick up a fuss?

The professor's last entry, written in a stilted scrawl, thanked all the members of his team, saying he couldn't have hoped to work with better. Having the dig taken away, just at the most exciting stage, was a huge and demoralising blow to them all, and they had done the only sane thing left under the circumstances, namely broken open the brandy and got royally drunk.

That was all. The remaining pages shouted blankly, devoid of the details of what happened after. Graham closed the journal and rubbed his eyes. It was later than he'd thought. Everything about the account indicated a major find, the discovery of the chamber, the proof the buildings were of religious significance. Something so notable ought to have resounded through archaeological circles, prompting papers and articles in various journals. But there had been nothing. How could such an important find go unreported? Even if the professor didn't feel he could publish anything with what they had they must have had pictures and notes at least. Why hadn't there been anything from the museum in Ankara? Was there some dreadful conspiracy to cover up the incident? A mutual agreement between Exeter University and the Turkish authorities to avoid an embarrassing academic scandal? It seemed highly unlikely. Did it relate to the professor's mysterious unpublished papers? In the light of what they had found, it was plausible. But then why did the professor decide not to publish, to meekly withdraw and go into retirement?

Over the next few evenings Graham did his own excavations, working methodically, digging through the boxes, reading through notes, journals and other documentation but found nothing else pertaining to the dig at Samuha. Not even photographs. Surely all of it hadn't been handed over to the Turkish inspector? Perhaps that material was still at Exeter University?

A week later, with much of the backlog of his own academic work cleared, Graham arrived at his college to find a letter waiting in his pigeon hole. He tore it open as he made his way up to his office and slipped the folded contents out. The letterhead bore the logo for Oxford Radiocarbon labs. It was from the man he'd spoken to on the phone, apologizing for taking so long getting back to him —claiming an unexpected surge in demand. The letter went on to say the reports commissioned by the professor for the date requested had been found and copies were enclosed. Graham looked the sheets over. The second page was a duplicate of the loose sheet he'd found in the professor's folder and, sure enough, he'd had the nacre on the big shard of pot carbon-dated. Then Graham read through the other sheets which had been included and frowned. Having reached his office he pushed the door shut with his heel and, still studying the reports, picked up the phone. He tried Rosetta's number again. Still no answer. He hung up, then made two more calls. One to Exeter and another to the British Museum.

4: Exeter

The students were mostly listening to Dr Bell's delivery, although one or two were checking their mobiles and writing texts. Par for the course these days. Graham had come in about half way through and taken a seat at the back of the lecture theatre. It felt a little odd, after all this time to be sitting alongside undergraduates in the same room where he'd sat listening attentively or, more often, inattentively, when he'd been an undergrad himself. A handful of the lectures had been given by the professor; he'd always paid attention in them.

Graham had driven down to Exeter in the morning and gone straight to the professor's house, in the hope Rosetta might answer the door, even if she wasn't answering the phone. Ringing the doorbell hadn't brought Rosetta, but the coffee-coloured cat he'd seen on his last visit had strolled out from under the bushes nearby and joined him on the doorstep. It had clearly decided he could be trusted after all, and that his legs were deserving of its affection. Just as Graham had been about to give up waiting, he'd heard crunching footsteps on the gravel of the driveway behind him.

A tall, Barbour clad lady of middling years had

approached.

"There you are Isis. Have you been up to your tricks?" she'd said, addressing the cat. "I'm supposed to be looking after her," she'd said to Graham, the last two words sounding like oftar har, "but she will insist on coming back here for mealtimes." She'd looked up at Graham. "Have we had the pleasure?"

Graham had suspected the cat was simply an excuse to pop over and check out the suspicious visitor who could have been casing the joint with a view to robbery. "Sorry, I'm Dr Chandlers. I'm... I was an old University friend of the professor's. I was wondering if Rosetta was around? I'm a little concerned, she hasn't been answering the phone and when I saw her after the funeral she was pretty upset about the loss of her father," Graham had said, putting his hand out. If that didn't allay the woman's suspicions he might as well have given up

and gone.

"Meredith Kendall." She'd stepped forward and given his hand a firm shake. "I'm afraid Rosetta has gone abroad for a couple of months." She'd stooped and picked up the cat. "Some kind of special travel agency."

"Is there any way I can get in touch with her? A

mobile number or something?"

"I've got the details at the house." Graham had been almost disappointed she didn't pronounce it hawse. "Do come over for some tea, Dr Chandlers." She, much like the cat, had clearly decided he was not a villain.

The remaining half-hour of Tinkerbell's lecture concerned the identification of pottery in Britain, from the Bronze Age through to the Dark Ages. It should have been a dull subject but, as well as being an expert in dating dig strata, Tinkerbell was also a good speaker and Graham found the little asides and anecdotes engaging.

"Twice in as many weeks, Dr C. I am honoured," said Tinkerbell, once all the students had filed out, leaving them alone.

"I know. People will start to gossip," Graham said, easing out of his seat and taking the steps down to where his friend was standing.

"So, presumably you're here for some unfinished business of the professor's, rather than anything actually work related? I take it for granted you've always lusted after my body and like spending as much time in my company as possible." Tinkerbell said, unplugging his laptop from the data projector lead and packing it into a canvas satchel. "Please tell me you aren't still trying to find out about that faked up shard of tourist tut?"

"No, not that. As a matter of fact, I was wondering if you still had that box folder from the professor's collection, if it contained the notes on those papers the professor didn't publish?"

"Sorry, it all got binned. There was nothing of interest, if it's any consolation."

Graham let out a sigh. "I don't believe you, Tink.

You're trying to hide something," he said.

"What you need, Dr C, is a pint or three –make you less crabby." Tinkerbell opened the door and gestured for Graham to precede him into the corridor.

"It's genuine you know," Graham said, as Tink followed him out. "The shard, that piece of tourist tut as you put it. The professor got it dated at the radiocarbon labs in Oxford, they still had the record. The thing is about 3300 years old."

"Great, you managed to prove the professor had at

least one piece of ancient crockery in his collection, well done." They continued out through the main doors and followed one of the many campus pathways.

"You knew, didn't you. Anyone else, any expert in the field, would have wondered about having a piece of pottery carbon dated instead of using thermoluminescence. You'd have said something when I mentioned it, but you already knew he'd had it done. How old it really was. What are you hiding, Tink?"

They stopped by a fishpond. A large koi carp turned just below the surface creating a ripple that spread in unhurried rings towards the edges.

Tinkerbell turned to Graham. "Look, we're both scientists. We propose hypotheses to explain the evidence and seek further evidence to corroborate them, and sometimes we get it wrong. Which is fine, disproving a hypothesis in favour of something better is also part of the scientific process. But..." Tinkerbell sucked air through his teeth. "...but if you try to supplant a whole group of well founded theories with one outrageous, unfounded theory, based on a single piece of circumstantial evidence, you'll get yourself labelled as a crackpot." Tinkerbell put his hand on Graham's shoulder. "The professor was under a lot of stress looking after the girl. If he'd published the paper, gone public with it all, he wouldn't just have shown himself to be a loony, he'd have cast the whole department into disrepute." Tinkerbell's great paw gave Graham a little shake. "Damnit, Graham! You, of all people, should know how tenuous the funding can be. If our most respected academic, our figurehead in the department here, had published that stuff, we'd all have been lucky to get work teaching in primary school. The professor, he just got a bit drawn in by..." He tutted, then looked at his watch and turned back towards the department building. "I've got to get on. Got a seminar group to mollycoddle. Sorry I don't have more time."

"I thought you said we should go for a drink?"

"I meant you. I'm working. It's all very well for Cambridge research fellows to go flitting about the country whenever they like, but I've got a teaching post. Trying to get some of the knowledge gleaned by generations of brilliant minds to stick in the sleep deprived, hungover or just plain thick, skulls of the current one." He walked away.

"But, what was it? What was the professor going to publish, that he'd have been prepared to risk his career over?" Graham called out.

"Stories, Graham, just a bunch of bedtime stories."

5: London

He'd always loved the British Museum. Graham remembered his father taking him there for the first time when
he was eight. A day spent being awed by the carved
faces of Greek heroes, entranced by the artistry worked
in Celtic and Saxon gold and fascinated by the Egyp-
tian sarcophagi and the dry mummified remains they
contained. Kings who'd lived their lives thousands of
years ago, yet physically there, close enough to touch, a
strange vibration spanning time, social standing and all
intervening events. A single day had only been enough
to see a part of the treasures the museum had to offer, but
it had been the day that would set the path of Graham's
future, the day he knew it lay in discovering the past.

Now he resisted the temptation to gawp, as many
of the tourists were doing, at the sight of the geometric
curves of the vast and unsupported roof of the Great
Court. He'd seen it all before, but it didn't lessen the
impact. Instead, he headed towards the circular Reading
Room building and climbed the wide steps curving
round the outside. They led up to a terraced café on the
next level. Gail was already waiting for him at one of the
café tables. A small woman in her mid forties, wearing

square-framed designer glasses, her pale brown curls held up by some kind of ornamental clasp. She was dressed smartly, as would be expected of an assistant director of such an institution. She stood as Graham approached and embraced him.

"Graham, it's lovely to see you. I'm sorry I couldn't see you sooner –terracotta warriors and delicate negotiations, you know the form." She let him go and indicated a seat. "Coffee?"

"Thanks, yes," said Graham.

Gail made a series of hand gestures to the young woman serving at the counter, while she continued talking to Graham. "Going to have to fly out to Beijing again next week." She'd always had an even tone that left the listener feeling she could be relied on; the sort of voice that, regardless of deadlines or chaos, would never be raised or panicked.

"I'm sure I remember you saying you were looking forward to the more sedentary kind of work the museum had to offer," said Graham.

Gail's mouth gained a rueful twist. "I did say that, didn't I? But it's worth all the running around. I love every minute. Anyway, how was the funeral? I'm so sorry I couldn't make it."

"It was fine, we all just ended up getting drunk with Dr Bell as expected, but it was a nice service, even if it was me reading the Eulogy. Some interesting additions from Alan's daughter, though." Graham raised an eyebrow. "Did you know she could speak Hattic?"

"So, you've met the inimitable Rosetta then? How is she? I haven't seen her since her eighteenth birthday. Is she still using a wheelchair and crutches?"

"No, she seems to be walking pretty well with the

aid of a stick. Though, I think her father's death has hit her quite hard. It's partly about her that I wanted to talk to you. Alan left me his journals, but they don't give the full story."

Gail sat back as the waitress approached their table and clinked a cappuccino in front of Graham.

"Thanks, Orla. Could you put it on the account please?"

The young woman nodded, gave a pleasant smile to Graham and returned to the counter.

Gail turned her attention back to Graham. "After you called, I had a look for any prints of the Samuha dig. As I told you, they must have all stayed at Exeter with the rest of the notes," she said, a wry smile tugging the corner of her mouth.

"But?"

"But, I'm a very organised individual. It was my responsibility to keep a record of the dig and the finds. Including photographic records. Which means I still had the negatives." She reached into the leather satchel beside her chair, took out a brown envelope and handed it to him. "We have an excellent photographic department here, I had them run off prints for you."

Graham shook his head as he took out the wad of black and white photographs and began leafing through.

"Gail, I hope they canonise you when you depart this Earth."

Gail took a sip of her coffee and put the cup down.

"I believe there's already a patron saint of lost causes."

The photographs showed the expected views of the site prior to any excavations. Then with dig and level markers in place and various shots of progress as levels were unearthed. There followed a series of close shots of finds, both in situ and on the workbench, with catalogue numbers on slips of paper beside each. Graham turned one to see if he could make out any of the cuneiform on a clay tablet.

"I'm sorry that the images of the clays aren't really detailed enough to read. They hadn't been cleaned up or anything."

"No, it's fine," he said, continuing to look through the photos. He stopped as the first image of the chamber came up. Just as the professor had described it in his journal, beautifully carved Hittite gods ranged around the walls picked out in stark relief by the camera flash and, dominating the centre of the image, the large earthenware vessel in its niche. He had to admit that it did look almost too perfect, but then, seeing anything intact and in situ at a site so ancient, was unusual enough to make it seem odd. He looked through the rest of the pictures, which showed various stages as the floor of the chamber was excavated. The last picture showed the broken stone covering from the niche after it had been turned over and placed so the fragments married up. On it was carved the image of the unnamed god, bending slightly to the right, one arm curved protectively over a kneeling female figure. Graham placed the pile of photographs on the table, this last image topmost.

Gail raised an eyebrow "What do you want to know Graham?"

"I've read through the professor's papers. All his field notes from Samuha. There seems to be an odd omission of any notes for his last, and unpublished, papers as well as a strange lack of other records of the dig. For example, what happened to the original photographs?

My contacts at Exeter are being oddly unhelpful in filling in the blanks. He tapped the top picture. "Anyone can see it had all the hallmarks of a major find, surely they would have kept some kind of records? Graham picked up the photographs again and shuffled back through them to a close shot of the earthenware pot in its niche. When I went to his house, there was this shard from a big earthenware vessel," Graham moved his hands apart to indicate the size, "looked remarkably like it could have come from something like this." He pointed back at the vessel in the photograph. "Though, on its inner surface it had unusual pearly glazing, very fake looking."

Gail nodded.

Graham looked her in the eye. "Turns out it's not, it's the real deal."

Gail looked around, "Okay, but not here," she said in a low voice.

That an assistant director of the British museum was a member of a club, should have come as no great surprise. The bow-fronted Georgian building was immaculately kept and, as far as Graham could tell, the internal panelling and various fixtures were original. The place reeked of established privilege and elitism. Gail secured a discrete corner booth and ordered a luncheon along with drinks for both of them. He was sure the costs of such an indulgence would have been eyebrow raising. He couldn't help wondering if he was missing out on some secret order of things. Perhaps he was being obtuse; living and working as a member of a college at Cambridge was to be part of one of the most elite and long established institutions in the world.

Graham picked through the crayfish tails in his salad.

"The last entries of the professor's field journal had all the details of the dig –how you discovered the chamber, the clays and the big storage vessel." he said "It also details the inspector from Ankara shutting you down. I know the professor stayed on in Istanbul for a few months after the rest of you. I now know he came back with a very sick child. But I want to know more. You were there Gail. What happened to your discovery? To the storage vessel? Why was nothing ever published? It wasn't like it was an insignificant find. I know the professor was preparing to publish a couple of final papers. I get the impression from Tink, he was dissuaded from doing so and any copies seem to have conveniently vanished. It's a lot to ask, but there's some connection between these things that I need to know."

Gail regarded him for a moment, swallowed her mouthful of trout and dabbed at her lips with her napkin. "You were right about the shard," she said. "It was part of the big storage jar we found in the chamber. I never thought it was a fake and nor did the professor –it was the implications of it being real no-one else could handle." She set her napkin down beside the remainder of her meal and leaned back on her seat. "We'd have missed any chance to study it further after the guy from the Ankara museum took possession of it, if it hadn't been for the earthquake."

"Earthquake, it doesn't mention anything about an earthquake in the journal?"

"I doubt it would. Things got a bit frantic on the last day. When the professor flew to Istanbul with the girl, he didn't have time to pack much. He left his journals behind."

Graham hadn't realised. He'd assumed the professor

had come across Rosetta later when he'd been staying in the city. A street kid or something. "So, you found Rosetta near the Samuha site? Was it the earthquake? Is that how she was hurt?"

Gail smiled. "Not exactly," she said, drawing out each word. "It was the last day and the people were due from Ankara later to take possession of the finds. We'd gone through a couple of bottles of Metaxa the night before, and I think we were all a bit worse for wear." She rolled her eyes. "I'd been up long enough to try making coffee. I thought it was the kettle boiling at first, just a rattling from the stove, but it built up as the earthquake hit. It wasn't enough to flatten houses or anything, but still, a strong tremor, which went on for a couple of minutes. They're pretty common in those parts, as you know, but no less unnerving. The gazebo where we'd been sorting the finds fell down, as did the back of the men's tent. Bit of a rough awakening –poor old Sam crawled out of it puking." Gail chuckled. "But when I checked on the professor, he wasn't there." She looked Graham in the eyes. "We'd joked about it the night before, but I thought it was only half serious. In hindsight, I like to think it was a reasonable thing to do. It was his dig and, damn the people at Ankara, he had a right to find out first."

"What?" said Graham.

"He'd got up early so he could find out what was in the pot, of course."

Graham laughed. "Fair enough, I suppose. If it was just going to be taken away from him. So what was in it, three-thousand-year-old wine?"

"You'd be surprised," she said, then frowned. "You're not recording this or anything?"

"Oh, good God Gail, as if I'd do something like that.

Look, I already know it's contentious from Tinkerbell's behaviour. I'm not out to damage anyone's career, least of all yours. Bloody hell. Just what was in the pot, Nazi gold?"

Gail took a sip of water from her glass and leaned closer "When I realised where he might be, I ran up there, worried he might have been hurt in the quake. There hadn't been a collapse or anything, but as soon as I entered the chamber I saw..." she paused, eyes focussed into the distance of memory. "The lighting stands had fallen over and gone out, though one was flickering a bit. It should have been pitch black, but the entire chamber was lit with a soft light. Most of the floor appeared to be covered in a silvery translucent liquid, but I swear it was where the light was coming from." Her voice, that reliable voice, became uncertain, "I can't really explain it, but it was beautiful and ... somehow it felt like love and comfort and protection." She focussed on Graham. "And in the middle were the remains of the vessel from the niche. It was smashed to pieces. The professor told me later, that at almost the same moment he'd unsealed the lid the quake had started and the vessel had lurched out of the niche." She glanced about again, then leaned even closer. "And within the remains of the pot was the girl. Lying there. She looked so emaciated and thin, I thought perhaps it was a cadaver. But the professor was trying to resuscitate her."

Graham frowned, "You're not trying to tell me she'd been in the storage vessel?"

"I can never say for sure, Graham. Only the professor knew what really happened, but she was there and she certainly wasn't in any state to have got herself there. I swear I heard one of her ribs break when he was giving her CPR. It worked though, he got her breathing."

"So, you're basically saying the girl –Rosetta, that is– for all intents and purposes appeared to have popped out of a three thousand year-old pot?" Graham sat back and tapped his fingers on the table. "Surely, she could have crawled into the chamber or been placed there during the night by her parents or something. Perhaps they saw a chance the rich English could help their sick daughter and set it all up?"

Gail checked there was no one in earshot. "I haven't talked about this with anyone before, and you can think I'm nuts if you like. But, in my opinion, she'd been in the vessel. She was still covered in the silvery liquid. The thing was, Graham, I got this feeling ... like a presence. Anyway as soon as she started breathing the glowing liquid started to disappear, to soak away into the floor of the chamber. I hate to say it, but like it knew what it was doing. By the time the professor and I had picked the girl up and started to carry her out of the chamber, it had nearly all gone. I went back later to check and there was no trace of it. The floor wasn't even damp."

She paused and studied Graham's face. He kept his expression neutral.

"I'm just telling you how I recall the events and what I experienced. You can interpret it any way you like," she said.

"From a lot of other people, I'd be sceptical, but I know you better. I know you're not the type to be subject to fancy.

"Thanks for the vote of confidence. It occurred to me to question if it was some kind of hangover induced hallucination, but the professor experienced the same thing. Also, the girl."

"What, she experienced it too?"

"No, she was completely unconscious. It was later. I'll get to that. Meanwhile we'd called in a medevac. We had an arrangement with the Turkish army, like a sort of insurance. They sent a helicopter and took the professor and the girl to the hospital in Istanbul. Admittedly the rest of us were then left to clear up. But before they took off, I took the liberty of putting a shard of the pot in the professor's rucksack. I figured we'd be unlikely to see the thing again and answers of some kind would be needed."

"So, that was the shard I saw at the professor's house. "

"I presume so."

"What happened to the rest of the vessel? Is it still in Turkey?"

"I had the pleasure of explaining things to a very irate man from the museum in Ankara later that day. I have to admit to doing nothing to assuage his doubts about the authenticity of the pot. Last thing I saw, when we'd packed up and were ready to leave, was some student bringing out the remaining shards just tossed in a cardboard box. Hardly the way one treats an irreplaceable ancient artefact. It's either in some basement of the museum, filed under F for folly, or it got thrown out with the rubbish. The guilt over which still makes me feel a little queasy when I think about it."

"So, a sick girl appears out of thin air and gets airlifted to hospital in Istanbul, weren't the Turkish authorities interested? You'd think they'd be trying to trace her parents or something?"

"You'd think. We talked to the teacher as well as the village guard in the local village. There weren't any children missing in the area. The Gendarmerie in the nearest town took records, but they knew nothing that could help. It got passed on to the police and other authorities in Ankara, with no results there either. No one had come forward about a missing girl in the area fitting her description." Gail paused and swirled the water in her glass. "To be honest, the authorities seemed more than happy someone else was dealing with it."

"Didn't Rosetta have anything to say? Surely, she could remember some details about where she came from, who her parents were?"

Gail looked into her water glass. "I'm going to have a glass of scotch. You want something?"

"Sure, yes, whisky sounds good. I'm getting the train back, so I'm not driving or anything."

"Good." She waved the waiter over, "Did Francis get any more of the Oban?" The waiter shook his head. "A couple of glasses of Talisker then."

The waiter nodded and headed off to the lower parts of the building.

"The girl hadn't regained consciousness when I got to Istanbul and went to see her at the hospital. It had taken us a couple of days to drive. The professor had been at her bedside pretty much the whole time. Poor mite, the doctors had never seen anything like it before. She wasn't malnourished as such, but a number of her bones had fused together and all her muscles were atrophied. When I got there, they'd moved her out of intensive care, but she was on oxygen, with various tubes coming out of her, as well as having both arms and legs in plaster. Most of her major tendons had become shortened. The doctors had to give her a number of operations just to get her out of the foetal position. Both wrists and a few ribs had been broken, probably when we gave her CPR ... Oh here we are," she said, as the waiter returned with a tray, cleared the plates and left a jug of water along with two crystal glasses of liquid amber.

"Do you want ice? I can get you ice if you want?" Gail said, picking up one of the glasses and appraising it with an expert's eye.

Graham shook his head, a pained look in his eyes. "So do they know what could have caused her to suffer such a condition?"

"No cause they could say for sure. The closest comparison was with the kind of problems that afflict astronauts after prolonged periods in space."

Graham almost choked on his first sip of whisky. "You're not going sci-fi on me, Gail? Aliens and archeology –been plenty of people trying to prove that one, but I wouldn't have thought to hear it from you."

"Aliens might be a more rational explanation." Gail took her glasses off and massaged the bridge of her nose. "The poor child regained a level of consciousness after a week, but she didn't seem aware of her surroundings. She was more stable at least, so the amount of tubes and wires reduced and the oxygen mask went. The doctors thought she might be brain damaged at first, but it was more like she was re-learning to use her senses. It was the professor who brought in the shard to show her. She didn't react at first, but when he put her fingers onto the glazing, she moved them, stroking the surface and smiling. And then..." Gail took a quick mouthful of her scotch and swallowed. "...then she whispered a word –the professor, the Turkish nurse, who was there, and myself– we'd all been so entranced by her stroking the glaze that we all heard it quite clearly– she said the word Ittraem."

67

Graham looked at her, "I heard her say the same word when she picked up the shard in the professor's house a couple of weeks ago. Do you know what it means?"

"I guess she does. When she started talking, we tried asking her all sorts, but no one could understand the language she was speaking. It wasn't Turkish or any of the regional tongues. The police even sent one of their translators to ask about her parents and how she came to be in Samuha, but he didn't have any luck. The only thing we learnt was that her name was Roth-té-ah –as best I can pronounce it– which quickly got mispronounced by everyone to Rosetta."

Graham smiled "Don't tell me, Hattic."

"It took another two weeks for the professor to figure it out. I'd had to fly back to the UK by then, but he'd stayed on. We spoke on the phone a couple of times. He'd told me of the eureka moment, when he'd realised she was speaking Hattic. As it turns out she could also read and speak a couple more ancient languages, Luwian and Akkadia, which is, at least, consistent with the time period. I think he was trying to get hold of you to translate, but you were on some dig in the middle of nowhere at the time. Got you to do a load of tapes and send them over.

Graham sat back and regarded her "Are you saying what I think you are saying here? Come on, Gail. You are an assistant director at the British Museum and here you are, pushing one of the worse gutter theories I've heard yet."

Gail shrugged, letting him draw his own conclusions.

"Isn't it possible that some small village in Turkey still speaks ancient Hattic. Tink said it – what if her parents saw the opportunity to offload their crippled daughter and somehow put her in the pot just before the professor arrived in the morning, or used the distraction of the earthquake to slip her into the chamber and lay her on the shards."

"What and chuck a few gallons of strangely volatile glowing liquid in there as well? Or perhaps the professor did it as a joke, just for me, so he could ruin a perfectly prestigious career. I've been through it all myself, all the possibilities." She shook her head, then took another mouthful of whisky, savouring its taste before looking him in the eyes. "Graham, I've only presented the facts as I witnessed them. You've found out for yourself about the dig and the authenticity of the pot. You need to draw your own conclusions, be a scientist, but keep an open mind. Occam's razor –the simplest explanation is most often the right one.

"Yes, but there doesn't seem to be any simple rational explanation, only complex irrational ones. It seems a little far-fetched to propose the ancient Hittites could have perfected a way to preserve their dead so they could be revived thousands of years later?"

"You're right, it does seem far-fetched, but it would explain her physical condition. Although, hypothetically, she would have needed to be alive for those physiological changes to occur. A sort of suspended animation. It would also fit with the way her hair and nails had grown.

Graham sat up straight, a look of consternation on his face. "What about her hair and nails?"

"When we found her she had hugely elongated fingernails, curling back on themselves, her hair as well. It was spread all around her, it must have been about six feet long ... is there something wrong, Graham?" she asked, noticing the consternation which had just jumped up and slapped him in the face.

He reached into his inside pocket and tugged out the folded documents, brought in case Gail had needed further evidence to get her to speak. He handed them over to her. She glanced at the cover letter and then examined the first report.

"I'd hoped he'd have that shard tested." She flipped back to the cover letter. "Carbon dating the glaze. Interesting. So the vessel really is, was, authentic."

"Look at the other report. The lab sent it along when I asked them for a copy of the report on the shard. He had it done at the same time. I hadn't appreciated the significance until you mentioned the length of her hair."

She flipped over to the next report, scanned through it and then with raised eyebrows read through it more slowly. Finally she looked back up at Graham. "I always knew he was a clever man, but I'd never appreciated quite how clever. To have the lab cut the strand into ordered sections. Anyone else would have just had the whole hair tested and got inconclusive results."

"Think about it Gail, if he had any hairs with the follicle attached, the DNA could have been tested and matched to Rosetta. He'd have incontrovertible proof. I think it's what his paper was about. It would have shaken archaeology, even our understanding of biology to the core. Why the hell didn't he publish? I can't believe he was persuaded not to publish by Tink and whoever else at the department in Exeter, for fear it might damage their chances of funding." He took a big gulp from his glass of scotch, finishing it, then coughed from the burning at the back of his throat.

Gail poured water from the jug into his empty glass

and proffered it, an expression of concern on her face as Graham swigged water until the fit abated.

"Thanks," he said, still hoarse.

"You know, I'm sure the professor had his own reasons for not publishing, even if it was caving in to pressure from his peers," Gail said, topping up her own water as she spoke.

"But don't you see, in all of archaeology, this is unique. Not just the phenomenon, but the opportunity it represents. A first-hand account of events from a witness who actually walked amongst the ancients, someone who lived during one of the earliest civilisations. There is so much we can learn, the benefits to our understanding of history would be enormous at the very least. Damn it! This is just too important a discovery to do nothing."

"Perhaps you need to step back and see this issue as a human being, rather than a scientist."

"How can I separate the two? The scientist gives me reasoning and rationality, the human gives me passion and drive. This issue clearly involves both. It is going to be hugely contentious and will put any number of people's noses out of joint." He looked at Gail's expression for a moment. "Oh, not you as well. Don't worry I won't implicate you or quote you in anything. Your job is safe."

"Graham, I'm central to the whole thing. It's not possible to do anything without implicating me in some way. But I think you are missing my point. I love my job, I really do, but it isn't the main issue here and if you can't figure that out I'm sorry for you."

She stood up and collected her satchel.

"Look, I'd best be getting back. Don't worry about lunch, it's already on my account here."

Graham stood up and shuffled out of the booth.

"Thanks, Gail. Not just for lunch, but filling me in on everything."

"Actually, it was rather good to finally talk it through with someone." She extracted herself and led the way to the door, giving a friendly wave to the waiter as she went. "Do you know what you are going to do now?"

"I can't just let it lie. I've got some research time accrued for my post. I think perhaps I need to seek out the source of all these questions before I decide what to do. Track down Rosetta herself. Ask her what ittraem means, amongst other things," he said, as they descended the stairs and headed through the hallway to the front door. Graham reached past her and held it open.

"Okay, Graham," she said, stepping out into the street. "But, truth-seeking aside, you'd better be damn sure you've got your ducks in a row before you go public with any of this. Be damn sure you actually want to." She carried on, over Graham's sounds of protest. "Just take some time to consider that the issue here lies between two schools of ethics."

With that she kissed him on the cheek, bid him goodbye and headed back towards the museum. Graham stood for a moment pondering, then headed for the nearest tube station.

6: Central Turkey

"Oh, we've been to most of the major sites," Deedee said, pushing a stray wisp of grey-shot hair back into its securing triangle of brown silk. Along with the pale linen shirt and matching shorts, she looked the part of a British explorer. "Mik never tires of it, do you dear?" She glanced over her shoulder to her husband.

Mik made an affirmative noise and continued setting out tiny cups on the table beside a plate of rich tea biscuits.

The site of Samuha was cradled in the lap of the impressive rock flanked hills behind. Their lower slopes, and the broad valley below, still clad in resilient spring grasses yet to be baked sere by the remorseless Turkish summer. It seemed Mik and Deedee had chosen to pitch the camp to look down over the site, mere piles of stone and hummocks in the ground. Features which, even an untrained eye could see, formed patterns that might once have been more.

A change in coughing sounds from the beautifully equipped kitchen tent indicated the promised coffee would soon be on its way. They'd got camping in comfort down to a fine art.

"What brings a young man like you all the way out here? I take it you're not in the medical field are you, Dr Chandlers?" Deedee said.

"Okay, you've got me, I'm an archaeologist. I'm very interested in the site professionally, but I also know your client, Rosetta Hargreaves, she's the reason I'm out here."

"A very clever young lady. It's normally us acting as tour guides for our clients, but she's so knowledgeable about the place. We've been treated to some fascinating insights. Haven't we Mik?"

"Yes, fascinating." Mik said, placing the coffee pot on a tray and carrying it over to where they were sat. "She's at some ruins, just up in the hills over there. But she asked to spend some time by herself this afternoon. We've left her to it. We've got the walkie-talkies if she needs anything."

They had got this all worked out to the tiniest detail. "I understand her father was a professor of archaeology?" said Deedee, pouring strong aromatic measures from the polished metal espresso maker.

"Yes, he was a good friend." said Graham.

Graham was aware he was undergoing a subtle interview as they talked and drank their coffees. The couple had a duty to protect Rosetta. Just another facet of their job, maybe? Although she did have a way of gaining champions amongst those who met her –the ones who unconsciously recognised how unique she was and who weren't terrified by it.

With their coffees finished Mik offered to take him up to find Rosetta, chatting amiably about the various sites they had visited as he puffed up the hillside. It seemed like a worthy business, they got paid on top of a free trip and their clients got to go to places their vulnerability or disability would otherwise prevent them from seeing. The combined experience of Mik and his wife offered escort, guide and travel service, along with catering and camping, where needed. They had jumped at the chance to take someone to a place further off the beaten track like Samuha: Mik admitted to being a bit bored with endless returns to Petra or the Valley of the Kings.

Rosetta was sitting on a stone block, not far from the remains of the temple site. Using a thick piece of charcoal, she was drawing with broad strokes in a large sketchbook. Yet another skill Graham had assumed she'd have trouble with, but perhaps the least surprising. She glanced up at Mik's hail, her eyes widening as she took in Graham. Dropping both charcoal and pad as she struggled to her feet, she put her hands to her mouth. Graham came to a stop, unsure of her reaction now the moment was upon them. But doubt evaporated as Rosetta dropped her hands to reveal a broad smile.

"I'll leave you two to it then," said Mik and, giving a nod to Rosetta, set off back down the hillside and left them alone with each other.

Graham had thought about what he was doing when he'd booked the flight, as well as on the journey itself. He'd thought hard about Rosetta and what she represented. He'd also thought about Gail's words.

He'd been pondering it all right up to the point when he'd left the main road from Ankara to take to the smaller roads leading to the ruins of Samuha. He'd wondered if he was doing the right thing. If using his research time to come out here chasing after the highly improbable was a foolish and damaging course. He'd believed that

Gail had been talking about the potential damage to their careers when she spoke about ethics and seeing the issue as a human being. The shock of true realisation made him pull over to the side of the road in a shower of dust and gravel. He'd sat staring at the undulating brown hills, examining and questioning his own feelings until a farmer pulled alongside in his truck to enquire if he had broken down. Graham had continued the journey with a head no longer conflicted and an expanded feeling within his chest.

He understood now why the professor had chosen not to publish his papers. Archaeologists rarely encountered this particular ethical dilemma. They were so used to dealing with people who had been dead long enough it didn't matter. But this instance involved a living, feeling person. A person who'd lost all they knew and loved, who'd already had to suffer God-knows what trauma. A person thrown into a frightening new world of convenience and technology, filled with strangers who spoke a different language. A fragile and very unique human being. It wasn't for the sake of anyone's career that the professor didn't publish his papers, it was to protect his adopted daughter from the world. She may well represent the greatest archaeological discovery in history, and the greater good may have been served by the revelations, but it would have to be at the cost of individual justice. The professor had made a choice, he'd kept her from all the exposure which would have come with publishing proof of her origins, out of love. What decent father wouldn't?

"I'm flattered you came halfway round the world to find me," she said.

She looked so exquisite standing there in a loose

cotton dress, her sable hair catching dark reds in the late afternoon sun. Those deep eyes that had seen such things. Graham gently clasped her hands in his.

"I'm ..." he started then, thinking for a moment, began again. "I prostrate myself with apology. I did not see your truth," he said, in slightly halting Hattic.

She laughed and replied in the same tongue, though all he could understand from the rapid and undulating flow was "You make words ... a great announcement."

"It seems like the student needs to teach the teacher," Graham said in English.

"If you want me to, I will."

"Yes, I would like that," he said. "Here, pull up a rock.

She sat back down and Graham picked up the sketchpad to sit beside her. He looked at what she'd been drawing, a tall, yet sturdy building with decorated rendering and a roof of stone slabs. He angled his head to look across the hillside at the few stones which remained to outline where buildings had once stood.

"Is this how it was?" he said.

"It's what I remember. There were flowering trees and bushes as well –we had water from the reservoir in the hills."

"It must have been beautiful."

"There were people too, lovely, ugly, happy, angry people. My people. I tell myself they lived full lives, but I keep coming back to the fact that they are all dead and long turned to dust. The beauty of this place is now in its silence, its loneliness."

"I'm sorry," he said. He understood now, there is a comfort in intimacy and an intimacy in comfort. This time he moved closer and took her in his arms. She returned the embrace and leant her head on his shoulder.

"You don't have to feel sorry for me,"she said "I've lived two amazing lives already and I'm only twenty-four."

Graham smiled. "Give or take a few millennia."

She meshed her fingers into his and brought his hand up to eye level studying it. "It's a long story." Her tone rose up as she spoke, suggesting an invitation rather than dismissal.

"I spoke to Gail Scott. She used to work with the professor. She was with him when he found you?"

Rosetta nodded. "I've met Gail a few times."

"She said one of the first words you said was ittraem. You said it to me when you thought I was going to pack the shard of pot for the museum. I'm assuming the shard is from the vessel the professor found on this site, is that ittraem?"

She smiled her enigmatic smile. "Ittraem is the name of an unnamed god of the underworld. He who could keep the earth-thunder in check."

"Handy to have around here. Seems like a contradiction though, how do you know his name if he is unnamed?"

Rosetta turned to look into Graham's eyes. "That, I can give you the short version of. It involves a girl, a young woman in those times, who was wed to a god. The king wanted to bring this god from another region and asked the priests to perform a ritual which would draw him here and make him wish to stay. The priests determined that if a young priestess of the area were offered as a bride the god would likely be tempted to do as the king wished. The girl they chose had been trained to her religious duties since she was a child and had reached the right age for the marriage. But the king wasn't happy with the ritual that was to be performed. He didn't just want the god to be wed, the girl might die or be unfaithful, and the god would leave. So he re-wrote the ritual to ensure she remained with the god within his embrace for perpetuity. Both god and bride were placed together in the same vessel and there they stayed, even after the king, the priests and the kingdom itself were long forgotten. But the god and his bride remained, and even though she wasn't conscious, she dreamed. She dreamed she was loved and cared for. And she dreamed a name: Ittraem."

Graham looked into her eyes with compassion and understanding. "I can't hope to compete with a god, Rosetta."

"I don't need a god, I need someone who can understand me."

Graham leaned closer, their lips almost touching. "In that case I know an eminent professor of paleolinguistics at Jefferson. I'm sure he'd be up for it. Mind you, he's in his eighties."

"Age doesn't always have to be a barrier. I don't mind men who are younger than me." she said with a smile curving her lips "Is he a good kisser?"

"I don't honestly know, I've never felt inclined to try."

Their lips brushed against each other then met and further words in any language became immaterial.

The End

Acknowledgements

Thanks to Dr Martin Gillard for his inside knowledge of archaeology departments.

Thanks to Viv Laine for her editing.

Thanks also to Otter Confusion for their input and encouragement.

Finally, thanks to Sanna, for her unceasing support.

Read the opening chapters of
Simon Cornish's latest novel

PAPER-FACE

With the expectation that Melanie wears a paper bag over her head in public, Paper-Face concerns the entwined narratives of a young woman and her father as they struggle to come to terms with life, the legacy of her mother's death, and each other. Written with wry humour and surreal touches, it is a story less about one person's difference, and more about what makes us all the same.

PAPER-FACE
Simon Cornish

1

It's not as if the start of my life was exactly auspicious, but then, it isn't as if I was born like other babies.

It's on VHS.

The delivery room has pale-brown walls that blend to oatmeal with the grainy image. The blinds are closed. Illumination comes from pinkish fluorescents and a stark medical theatre light above. Anonymous plastic-aproned staff stand around the bed, murmuring words of encouragement; words uttered so many times, to so many mothers, they mean nothing.

I'm pretty sure she isn't listening anyway.

The bed is propped up at an angle and upon it is my mother, Yvette Desireux. Dark locks sweat-bedraggled, her beautiful, iconic face churned to travesty as she breathes heavily, bearing down on the slick ball of flesh between her spread legs. Flesh that is not hers, but of her. The motion of the camera is unnerving: switching from this intimate repugnancy back to my mother's face, dodging round medical staff, zooming close, then out for a wide shot, the focus reeling to keep up. Throughout, my father's commentary from behind the camera is a combination of banal and unnecessary observations, interspersed with animated exhortations to my mother. At some point he gets mixed up, telling the stretched anatomy between her raised thighs she's doing really well, nearly there now, then turning back to my mother's face to inform her clinically that the vagina is fully dilated. Over ten centimetres. To which she shouts:

'Youdon'thavetotellmeit'sfullydilated, I can fucking feel it!'

She draws a breath, then, looking into the lens, straight at my father, she screams the most creatively improbable string of invective at him. Telling him what he can do with his camera. All in French, no stopping. She continues for a good few minutes without pause. I still feel uncomfortable watching TV, but this is worth it, just for that bit. Even though he can barely follow the simplest part of such vilification, it's clear he gets the underlying meaning. The camera becomes steady, held at a slight angle, but still pointed at her face. As it holds there, the diatribe finishes and she draws a long, deep breath. A wide smile curls across her lips. A smile of victory. Perhaps, because she's just given birth or, perhaps wickedly, because she has managed to distract my Dad long enough to prevent him getting it on tape. But that was my mother: there was no denying she could capture an audience.

At this point a voice from one of the midwives, off-camera, says he might want to stop filming for a bit.

'The afterbirth,' she says.

The tape flicks to static for a moment, then resumes. The camera has been positioned to point at the bed. My father, Dominic Rose, comes into shot, backing away. A grin opens the corner of his mouth as he winks at the lens. Six foot two and raffishly handsome. A little less craggy than he looks these days but not much. He seats himself on the bed beside my mother, takes her hand and kisses it. They look right together.

The room has changed a little. The staff have all gone, the big light has been turned off and I guess the blinds have been opened, as crisp shadows now underpin the items in the room. The bed has been altered so my mother is propped up more comfortably against some pillows. They both keep looking towards the doorway.

I've watched the tape a few times. Not to see myself coming out or anything weird, but to see the expressions on my parents' faces in the moment that follows, the moment the consultant comes in and tells them the medical explanation, the moment he says the word 'different'.

My father is easy to read: the proud smile disappears as his mouth gradually falls open and the tiniest crease puckers up between his eyebrows. He slowly turns to look at my mother, that tiny crease of his now emanating a tragic compassion.

My mother is harder to figure. Still pale and exhausted from labour, she is holding a small compact as she re-applies her lipstick. When the consultant begins to speak, she holds the lipstick away from her. While she listens it stays there, sticking upright like a red finger. Her expression remains unchanged throughout. Then, just as my father turns to look at her, she closes her eyes for a moment, too long for a blink, and opens them again.

Shock, detachment, or the rallying of steely self-control?
I've never been able to tell.

2

Melanie sat cross-legged in the space between the metal racks, pulling out box after box from the lowest shelves and checking their contents; not so much a stock take as a cull. The storeroom was a squalid grotto of mixed-up inventory, line ends and returns, lit by a single yellowish bulb, too stingy to cast its illumination as far as the corners. Smells of new dye and mildewed carpet competed for dominance, only to be undermined in places by a more insidious, musky odour best not dwelt upon.

The previous evening's furore—the accusations, the flaming—still felt raw around and behind Melanie's eyes. She pushed a box of key fobs back into place, shoving it harder when it stuck and making them jangle in protest. She should never have listened to Marsha. No, that wasn't fair. Marsha was right; she should have been upfront about having a difference from the outset. The rules of the online forum, on which she'd been an active participant for over a year, had been strict about using a real photograph of yourself. Using an old photo of her mother had been dishonest. But then she might not have garnered such attention from the others on there, might not have attracted the increasingly intimate attention of SamIAm, one of the admins. That their online relationship of the last four months had exploded last night was probably inevitable. What is the next step after you fall in love online? He was so insistent about wanting to meet in the flesh. They had even talked about a future together, holidays, houses.

In the space of a few hours her online haven had turned into a bloody theatre of accusations, allegations and insults. Melanie bit her lip; she'd been responsible for some of the worst flaming. Any bridges left by those who had been sympathetic were likely to be ash now. She would have to find another forum and start over. But was it even worth it?

She inspected a box of T-shirts printed with the faces of a voguish indie band from the nineties. Ragged holes now peppered most of them. The plastic wrappings had been left open leaving the cloth exposed to the moths. She examined one of the miniature papery casings with its tiny larva living inside. If it could be called living: hiding in its little grey bag, in an old tour shirt, in a box, waiting to turn into a dull papery moth. The comparison did not escape her. She flicked it away and pushed the box to one side.

The next box contained loose hoody tops and, as she discovered, pink and helpless in their folds, a squirming nest of baby rats. While Melanie wasn't one to run screaming at the sight, she did wonder where the parents might be. She eyed the darker shadows beneath the shelving for signs of furry motion before getting up to punch open the fire door to the yard at the rear of the shop. At least they'd have the option of moving out—if Whit didn't find them first.

Whittington, to give him his full name—white and black, daytime scatter-cushion and nocturnal serial killer of all local wildlife smaller than his deceptively fluffy bulk—was partial to rats. But, much like Melanie's father, he would be unlikely to get up before lunchtime today.

Real daylight edged its way in from the open fire door and as she turned back to the room, her eye was caught by something which would have been impossible to spot in the normal gloom. Something tucked away on one of the top shelves against the inner wall. Something printed with the word URGENT. Climbing onto the lowest shelf, Melanie could just reach, and with two deft fingers pulled down the stash of envelopes. Several had been opened, though the latest, which from the post-date had only arrived five days ago, was still sealed.

''Scuse me, you got any more of these bags? I'm looking for one in black.'

The words made her jump. A customer stood framed in the doorway leading to the shop. A guy, faded T-shirt and torn jeans, cute in a grungy sort of way. Melanie must have missed the buzzer while she was at the back.

'Like this?' He held up a green canvas Pearl Jam satchel. 'But in, oh...'

He trailed off, trying to look anywhere but at Melanie.

Bag! It had been in the way when she'd been looking through the stock; she hadn't expected anyone to catch her in here without it. She scrambled back to where she'd been sitting, dropping the letters and pulling curtains of dark hair over her face.

'Just a second,' she said, rummaging through the detritus she'd created earlier. At the bottom of the pile, she found what she was looking for: a simple, brown paper-bag with two holes cut in it for her eyes. A little crumpled now but not torn. She opened it and slid it over her head, the familiar rustling a calming comfort. It wasn't one of the more presentable bags she'd started designing for herself, but it was functional. As she aligned the eye-holes, she noticed a single, black, Pearl Jam satchel on the shelf in front of her.

'You're in luck, there's one left,' she called out. Mindful of the various obscured hazards now littering the floor, Melanie picked her way carefully from the back of the room holding the satchel by the strap.

'Sorry, I didn't realise,' the guy said, as Melanie emerged, 'I wasn't taking the piss or anything. I didn't notice you was different... I mean, I do actually want to buy the bag... shit, I mean the Pearl Jam one.' Colour started blotching his cheeks. It made him look even cuter.

She'd only just finished with SamIAm and she was eyeing up guys already. Admittedly he was out of her league, if she was even in one. He probably had a girl-friend, an attractive, normal girlfriend; someone who had the right clothes, the right job; someone real who could go out into the world confident with who she was.

Melanie let the guy's embarrassment diffuse her own. The barrier was there now, a thin layer of stiffened paper.

In the end he bought a poster as well. Not that Melanie would ever play the diff card, but if he wanted to talk his way into buying more while he tied himself into politically correct knots, she wasn't going to talk him back out of it. She pretended to be busy looking through some ancient and unsaleable band-badges in the drawers beneath the counter until she heard the shop door click closed behind him, then stepped back into the stockroom, retrieved the letters and began to read.

3

The blissful amnesia of night unravelled as the invading harpy desecrated the musty, used-smoke sanctity of Dom's bedroom.

'For goodness sake, Dad! Why'd you let it get into such a state without telling me?' the harpy said.

Dom heard the rustle of paperwork as the tirade continued.

'Didn't you stop to think, for just the teeniest moment, that if we didn't have enough money a year ago, how borrowing more would make us better off?'

It was too early in the day to be dealing with this; it seemed unfair not to have some kind of run-up. Perhaps it would go away if he kept his eyes shut.

'It wouldn't have been as bad if you hadn't kept it all hidden. Did you think it would all just disappear into the financial ether? More than half is their bloody fees. And what are chattels, for goodness sake?'

The screeching of curtain rings under duress was too much to take and Dom, giving up on any chance of continued sleep, opened his eyes. Rolling stiffly onto one elbow, he ran his fingers through his tousled auburn hair and yawned.

'And a good morning to you too, Melanie. What's the time?' He hauled himself higher, showing the intricate Celtic designs winding in fading black across the well-defined topography of his left shoulder and upper arm. He reached for a glass on the bedside table, inspected it and, finding it empty, put it back. 'There's no chance of a coffee is there, love?'

'Are you listening, Dad? The loans?' Mel threw the letters down onto the bed.

Dom sighed. 'Look, petal, we needed to buy more stock. And it helped with the mortgage.'

'Don't look petal me! You can't take out a loan to make repayments for another loan. It's a vicious circle.'

'There was your laptop.' His second foray onto the bedside table yielded a cigarette. 'Chuck me that lighter from the chest of drawers, will you, poppet?'

Mel turned and rummaged through the guitar tuners, assorted novels, philosophy books and tour souvenirs.

'Here,' she said, throwing the silver Zippo.

He caught it fluidly with one hand and began the flourish of clicks and flicks that resulted in a lit cigarette—followed by a spasm of phlegmy coughs.

'Look, the shop's been doing considerably better with the new lines in last few months. We had to pay for them somehow.' he said, trying not to croak.

'Yes okay, we needed stock.' She waved her hands. 'Although it's not like we managed to sell half of it before the rats got to it, but even with my computer, it hardly accounts for twelve grand.'

'We need to live as well, poppet.' He coughed again.

'We had bills, insurance and shopping and... stuff.' He narrowed his grey eyes. 'Rats?'

'Yes, and moths. But twelve thousand pounds? I don't know how we can afford to make the payments. Though it might be easier if you didn't spend most of what we have on cigarettes and booze.' She kicked an empty bourbon bottle under the bed, which made clinking sounds as it settled amongst its predecessors.

Dom tilted his head forward and to one side, looking up at her with one raised eyebrow.

'Okay, okay. I'll start smoking rollups.'

Mel let out a breath and put her hands on her hips.

'The puppy dog look isn't going to work on me this time, Dad. Come on, this is serious. That last letter, if you'd bothered to open it, is from a firm of bailiffs,' she said. 'If we can't get them some kind of payment on Monday, they're going to come and seize stuff.'

Crap, the devil must have invented white envelopes just to torture people. 'It's fine, they're just rattling sabres.' Dom ran his fingers through his hair again as he considered, trying to think up to her speed. 'I was going to go to the bank first thing on Monday anyway. I'll see if I can get them to re-mortgage the flat.'

'Mortgages take time to process, don't they? Every delay just ends up costing more. They're going to want the money as soon as possible. These people aren't messing about! And I'm supposed to go to France next month.'

She sat down on the end of the bed and slid her bag off. She was frowning, a little furrow between her eyebrows, doubtless mirroring his own. He rubbed his fingers across his forehead, making smoke trails from his cigarette.

'Look, poppet, I'll talk to them about extending the overdraft until this month's mortgage goes through. Don't worry, it'll be fine.'

'Please don't mess it up, Dad.'

'One way or another, we'll get it sorted. Now how's about you rustle up a drink for us,' he said, smiling.

Mel made an exasperated noise. 'What did your last slave die of?'

The retort hung awkwardly for a moment.

Dom reinforced the corners of his smile. 'Beaten to death for impertinence,' he said. The void within there as ever; some wounds could never fully heal.

Mel picked up her bag and moved towards the door.

'I'll put the kettle on,' she said.

About The Author

Working as professional animator, scriptwriter and illustrator for most of his career, Simon graduated with an MA in Professional Writing from Falmouth University in 2011 and has been working on script and prose writing since.

Simon's story *And God Said* was published in the 2010 Fish Anthology as a runner-up in the One-page Fiction Prize. His spoof article *The Hemmingway Virus* won the Brighton COW Spring Break non-fiction competition in 2011 and his short story *The Words* was a runner up in the Fish Short Story Prize, getting an honorary mention and has been published as part of the 2014 Fish Anthology.

In addition to his own writing, Simon has edited and published *Between Stops* an anthology of short edgy fiction from several new writers.

Printed in Great Britain
by Amazon